LET THEM ALL STARVE

Alexander Barrie has written for the *Reader's Digest*, *Sunday Times* and *Daily Telegraph*.

During the Second World War he was a pilot with the RAF. He has flown all the light aircraft that appear in the *Jonathan Kane* books and has received full cooperation from the RAF in his research into military planes and equipment.

Alexander Barrie

LET THEM ALL STARVE

cover illustration by C L Doughty
text illustrations by Paul Wright

Piccolo
Pan Books London and Sydney

First published 1975 by Frederick Muller Ltd
This abridged edition published 1977 by Pan Books Ltd,
Cavaye Place, London sw10 9pg
© Alexander Barrie 1975
isbn 0 330 25073 6
Printed and bound in Great Britain by
Richard Clay (The Chaucer Press) Ltd, Bungay, Suffolk

CONTENTS

For Keene Langhorne of Pan Am
and Riddle Field

Once again I have been greatly helped by my young editorial advisers, and my thanks go specially to David Rafique, David Wood and Graham Butcher. I am also much indebted again to John Willis of Trans Europe Air Charter Limited for valuable and patiently given advice. Lastly, thank you to my own family—particularly Christopher and Alison.

INTRODUCTION

In Jonathan Kane's view, the only proper way to spend time off from school is at Lonehead Airfield, not very far from Burton-on-Trent, England. Here, Peregrene Langhorne runs a small air charter business, helped by his girlfriend, Roz, and by Charlie Thompson, Chief Instructor at the Mid County Flying Club.

Jonathan's role is to wash down the aircraft, taxi them here and there—and fly whenever he gets a chance—and the chances come quite often. He is $13\frac{1}{2}$ years old, likes to think he looks older (which in truth he doesn't), is 5 feet 1 inch tall, dark haired, even-featured and has intelligent brown eyes and a ready smile. Almost everybody likes him. Much of the time his is a happy child, but he does have self-pitying moments, and he certainly knows what it is to feel afraid.

Henry and Elizabeth Kane, Jonathan's tolerant parents, accept the fact that, at least at this stage in his life, their son is wholly engrossed in aviation and his Lonehead friends. I suppose you could say they are ideal parents for an adventurous boy—there when they're needed but not possessive or seeking to change him. They understand what Jonno is up to; that he is taking his place in an adult world, striving to stand on his own still quite small feet, and most of the time (not always) making a very good go of the attempt.

They are a proud lot at Lonehead: Independent,

free, running their own show, making decisions, working and playing hard, taking risks, trusting each other and living an outdoor, man's world of adventure. Not the easiest people to keep up with.

I must say I like and admire them all, and of them all, I like and admire Jonathan the most.

A.B.

Chapter One

WALLY SPELLS IT OUT

The big car came up the approach road, rolled on to the field and kept coming, pushing through the wet grass towards Golf Alpha Romeo Yankee Foxtrot, the old twin-engined Aztec B. Jonathan Kane paused on the wing watching. That was a Wankel-engined NSU Ro80 – a new one and some car. It was out in the middle now, right in the middle of runway one-one and doing maybe 20 miles an hour – an extraordinary sight and irregular to say the least. Jonathan's big, bright brown eyes grew bigger still with surprise.

Unexpectedly the car swung hard right and stopped just a foot or two away from Yankee Foxtrot's port wingtip. There was a woman at the wheel. The car window was throwing up reflections of the sky which made it difficult to see inside, but there was a grey-haired woman there, and she looked on the fat side. Jonathan hopped off the wing and walked over to the driver's door. She spoke first.

'Not exactly Heathrow or La Guardia, is it?'

'Eh?'

She waved a pudgy hand and laughed. 'Not the biggest airport in the world. On the small side in fact.'

Jonathan recovered himself. Looking as dignified as his thirteen years would allow, he waggled an admonitory finger at the lady. 'You're not supposed to drive on the runways,' he said. 'It's a very dangerous thing to do.'

9

The lady stopped laughing. 'Runways, *runways*.' She gave a forced little laugh. 'I don't seem to see any runways. And, anyway, don't be impertinent. What's your name?'

Jonathan flushed and scowled at the lady, who was looking very regal now and disdainful. So far she was well ahead on points. 'I'm Jonathan,' he said, 'and please remember not to drive on the runways in future. This is a grass runway here and that' – he pointed into the distance – 'that's another one, two-two.'

She put her hand out of the window and reaching round behind him slapped him on the back of the head. 'Don't talk to me like that,' she said, 'you silly little boy.'

A flood of anger began to race through Jonathan like a mountain river and then, before it spilled over into action, the lady laughed again; or perhaps chuckle describes the sound better – a bit less than a laugh.

'Let's not fight,' she said. 'I'm Mrs Kidwallader Jones. *The* Mrs Kidwallader Jones. You've heard of me?'

'I know who you are now. You've come to see Perry.'

'I've come to see Mr Peregrene Langhorne.' The regal look was coming back. 'I have an appointment to discuss chartering his aircraft. Where shall I find him?'

Jonathan gestured towards a hangar, a shade dilapidated in appearance, with patches of rust in the corrugated sheets that clad its walls. 'I think he's in the tower. See the window in the top of the hangar there? He's up there, I think. You can drive over and park by the bowser.'

'Hop in,' she said, opening the door on the passenger's side. Jonathan walked round the back of the car and hopped in. Mrs Kidwallader Jones went off with

a powerful surge that had the back wheels spin
and turves flying into the air.

Charlie Thompson was in a pretty bad mood that
day. One of those black moods had settled on him like
an evening mist, and Roz and Perry had wisely been
leaving him alone until the gloom blew away, as it
always did in the end. He looked sourly over towards
the plump lady and tugged at his ragged, red moustache disapprovingly.

Roz jumped up from her stool and switched on that
bewitching smile that always seemed to be on hand.
'I'm Rosemary-Anne Hart,' she said. 'Er, Roz. You'll
be Mrs Kidwallader Jones. Do come in.'

'Well *that's* a better reception. I must say I'm
glad ...'

As Mrs Kidwallader Jones was starting on her little
speech the radio crackled into action. 'Lonehead.
Cessna one-fifty Golf Bravo Alpha Mike X-ray from
Biggin. Good morning. Estimate you eleven-fifteen.
Request landing instructions.'

Roz looked quickly at Charlie, then switched her
glance to Jon. 'Deal with it, Jonno, will you?' she said
and went over to shake hands with the visitor.

Jonathan pressed the transmit button. 'Mike X-ray.
Lonehead. Good morning. Land at your discretion.'

Mrs Kidwallader Jones' voice was rising now and
booming across towards the microphone. 'Stand by,'
said Jonathan briskly, then released the button. This
time he shouted across at Mrs Kidwallader Jones.
'Look,' he yelled, 'I can't hear myself talk. Will you
please shut up!' It was her turn to look surprised. She
gulped in a big breath to make a fighting reply when
Roz, still smiling and cool, held a finger up to the lady's
lips. 'Shh,' she said. At that Charlie managed a hint of

a grin, the first sign of humour from him that morning.

Jonathan pressed the button again. 'Mike X-ray. Lonehead.'

'Go ahead Lonehead.'

'Mike X-ray. You are cleared to land at your discretion. Runway two-two. QFE niner niner niner.'

Jonathan released the button and turned to face Mrs Kidwallader Jones, who was standing just inside the doorway looking as if she'd swallowed a hard-boiled egg whole.

'You are a very rude little boy – a very silly *little* boy,' she said, emphasizing the 'little' which she clearly thought would hurt most. 'You need a thorough spanking, that's what. Before you're much older I'll have you across my knee, you wait and see.'

'Across your knee?' retorted Jonathan. 'I wouldn't be able to get on it for your big . . .'

Roz started the shush-shush noises again before he finished his sentence. The boy was flashing with anger now, his eyes sparkling and his cheeks in full colour.

'Shush, shush, shush. Please, everybody,' Roz spoke gently, soothingly. 'Let's calm down and have a cup of coffee.' A big smile had spread across Charlie's face, and he nodded and winked at Jonathan.

Roz plugged the kettle in and pulled a chair out for Mrs Kidwallader Jones, who settled herself on it majestically. 'Where is Mr Langhorne?' she asked.

Somebody was coming up the stairs whistling. 'I think that's him,' said Roz.

Perry ambled through the door. 'Morning all,' he said and gave a little nod towards the lady visitor. 'Hi. I'll have it black thanks Jonathan.' He walked over to the window and looked out across the rolling countryside. 'Uhuh, that's a front coming through. More rain. Uhuh.' He sat down on one of the stools. In moment Jonathan handed him his coffee.

The battle glint which had been dying in Mrs Kidwallader Jones' eyes began to come back. 'Mr Langhorne,' she said icily, 'do you mind taking some notice of me?'

'Oh sure. I'm sorry. How are you, Mrs Jones?'

A look of irritation swept across her plump face. 'I'm not here to discuss my health. I'm here to talk business.'

Perry didn't react at all at first, then suddenly flicked his gaze across to look at her. Perry had a way with him, a presence about him that made everyone take notice. Mrs Kidwallader Jones was getting the full Langhorne voltage right now as he studied her with clear grey eyes set in a weathered, lean face. She looked all wrong sitting there in the tower of Lonehead field – white hair, lined features, big breasts, thick waist, fat knees and funny little feet. Her clothes strained round her and you would have thought that the buttons were wired on. She had four rings on her fingers, big expensive-looking jobs.

'Okay, Mrs Jones. Talk away.'

She got down to it. 'I am Mrs Patricia Kidwallader Jones. My husband, Franklyn, was Chairman of the Basitto Mines Corporation. He died, poor man. It was sudden. Years ago. Anyway, I am rich, really very rich. Have you ever been rich, Mr Langhorne?'

Perry looked for a moment as if he wasn't going to reply, then sipped his coffee and murmured, 'No.'

'Well, it's very pleasant. I give away a great deal of money to the poor, but I'm not silly about it. I have no intention of being poor myself. Can you understand that?'

'Sure.'

'Two years ago I founded a movement, a charity, called Save Mambay. Sir William Krier, an old friend of Franklyn's, helped me. I put £50,000 of my own money into it and we've raised another quarter of a million by campaigning. Mambay is in North Africa as I imagine you know. A delightful country decimated, absolutely *decimated* by droughts. Awful to hear of the children dying. Franklyn was very fond of Mambay. I felt I owed it to him to do something, to try to help. Mambay is poor you know. There wasn't any leeway left. When the rains stopped coming people just died. Just died.'

'I remember the news reports.'

'We've been sending food consignments out to Mambay, but something's going wrong. The people who need it aren't getting it. That's why I'm talking to you.'

'Uhuh.'

Charlie spoke. 'Quite right too, Mrs J,' he said. 'Peregrene here's very strong on charities. Very keen. You should just see him open a bazaar. Forty people got arrested at the last one.'

Mrs Kidwallader Jones turned to wither him with a look which, although it came from eyes that seemed a little on the small side, had a considerable glitter and zoink to it. 'And who exactly are you?' she asked icily.

Charlie stood up. 'I'm a steam engineer. Have you seen any? Steam I mean. Blowed if I can find it.' He crouched down to look under the desk.

'That's Charlie Thompson,' explained Perry. 'He's Chief Instructor here and not as bad as he looks.'

'I should certainly hope not.'

'You don't have to laugh at his jokes.'

'I certainly shan't. I must say you have some very rude friends, Mr Langhorne.' She had switched her

15

glittery look to Jon as she finished the sentence.

Roz began to walk round picking up the coffee cups. 'Don't do that,' commanded Mrs Kidwallader Jones. 'I don't like to see women waiting on men. Let them do it for themselves. I'm very strong on women's lib you know. Time we fought back. The boy can do the washing up.' Jonathan went red again from embarrassment and anger and seemed about to speak.

But Roz saved the situation again with her sparkling smile. 'Really, Mrs Kidwallader Jones. I don't mind,' she said, and carried on gathering up the cups.

'Well it's time you did.'

'Mrs Kidwallader Jones – shall we go back to talking business? I'm real busy so let's get down to it. Just what do you want from me?' Perry's voice had gone very flat and gave the clear impression that the lady's time was fast running out. Evidently she hadn't noticed.

'You're American, Mr Langhorne, or you've been there! I can trace a little burr in the way you speak. How nice. I like Americans, generous people – well, some of them are – quite remarkably so.'

Perry got up from the stool and moved towards the door. 'I guess I have to leave now,' he said. 'I'm needed down in the hangar.'

Mrs Kidwallader Jones struggled on to her little feet too. 'No, please,' she said. 'I won't waste any more time. Just give me two more minutes. Please.' A victory to Perry. He sat down again, but his expression had dulled a bit and you got the feeling his mind had largely switched off. Like waiting in a traffic jam.

'Thank you. Thank you so much.' Mrs Kidwallader Jones settled carefully back into her chair and turned a motherly smile towards him. 'Now, I've made in-

16

quiries,' she went on, 'many of them. And I've asked for help. And it isn't doing any good. The vital food supplies just aren't getting through. I don't know what happens to them, but there's corruption in the picture somewhere.'

Peregrene seemed a shade more interested. 'Who've you spoken to about it?' he asked.

'Well, I've been to the Foreign Office. A very tiresome man there spoke to me as if I were a little girl of ten; almost patted me on the head; seemed ready to do anything except something useful. When I left I made it plain what I thought of him all right.' She gave a little cackle of a laugh at the recollection.

'Then I went to the Registrar of Charities. Not interested. "Try the Mambay embassy," the man said. So I went there. A young man said he'd make inquiries for me. Months passed, and I phoned and phoned. At last they told me the food was getting through as planned – nothing to worry about. What rot!'

'But how do you know the stuff isn't getting there?'

'Because I can't get any evidence that it *is*. I mean, you'd hear wouldn't you? People still die. Everyone you speak to seems so vague.'

'And what about this guy – what's his name? Krier? What's his view?'

'Sir William? Oh, he says to stop worrying. He thinks everything's all right. Men!' she added bitterly. 'So long as their own stomachs are full it's all right. Well, it's *not* all right. And beside, a friend of mine actually saw one of our food containers in a completely different part of Africa – miles and miles from Mambay.'

'Have you told Krier?'

'Yes. He doesn't believe it. Thinks my friend made

17

a mistake. Anyway, I want to go out to Mambay to have a look for myself, and I'd like you to fly me there.'

'Use an airline,' suggested Perry. 'If I go it'll cost you a thousand pounds. Maybe two.'

Mrs Kidwallader Jones straightened in her chair and tilted her head back proudly. 'Mr Langhorne, I don't mind if it's five,' she said. 'The cost doesn't matter.'

'How long d'you want to be there?'

'I haven't the slightest idea.'

'Say a week?'

'Perhaps.'

'What d'you think, Charlie?' asked Perry.

'The way things are going, I think we're just the team the lady needs,' replied Charlie. 'A little cash in advance and we say yes, I think.'

Suddenly Mrs Kidwallader Jones was looking a lot less happy. 'Are you suggesting that he comes too?' she asked, giving a nod of her head towards Charlie's corner of the room.

'Sure. I'll need him,' said Peregrene.

'And me,' added Jonathan brightly.

'Oh, my lord!' murmured Mrs Kidwallader Jones. 'I've no wish to have *their* company for a week.'

'Don't be so sure,' said Charlie amiably. 'I grow on people.'

Mrs Kidwallader Jones didn't soften. 'So do warts,' she retorted. 'Anyway, the boy's too young.'

'He generally comes,' said Perry. 'He's real useful too.'

Mrs Kidwallader Jones considered the situation for half a minute or so in silence, rubbing the thumb and fingers of her right hand together with the agony of thought.

'All right,' she said at last. 'I'll agree on one condition. That you, my dear, come too.' She was looking at Roz, and softening as she spoke.

'Me?' Roz looked startled. 'I don't usually go on these trips. I mind the field here.'

'I insist. Positively insist. If that man and that boy are going, so are you. What about it?'

'Rubbish,' said Charlie. 'This isn't the sort of scene for a woman.'

'Oh? Really? And what d'you think I am then?'

Charlie ran a candid eye over Mrs Kidwallader Jones' fleshy form. 'Don't make me answer that, ma'am,' he said.

Peregrene ambled over to Roz. 'How d'you feel about it, Roz?' he asked. 'I don't see why you shouldn't come if you like to.'

'All right, why not? This once I will. I'll come. It's a deal.'

Mrs Kidwallader Jones settled back more comfortably in her chair. 'Good, good,' she said. 'We'll show them, we women. Now, we're going to see a lot of each other, so let's be less formal. I'll call you Roz in future.'

'Yes. Of course. Please do – er, Patricia.' Roz felt and looked embarrassed. 'That is right, isn't it? – you are Patricia.'

'No. Yes and no. It is my name, but I don't want you to call me that. You can call me' – she smiled coyly, a smile that brought incongruous dimples to her plump cheeks – 'you can call me Wally. You all can,' she added, flooding the room with goodwill. 'Even you, Jonathan.'

An awkward silence followed, and then Charlie sniffed loudly. Jonathan felt he perhaps ought to say something, since he'd been specially named and, anyway, the old girl was looking at him. 'Thanks,' he mut-

19

tered and reached into a battered dresser for something to drink. He pulled a bottle out and began to open it.

'What's that?' With startling suddenness Wally seemed to have reverted to being the battling Mrs Kidwallader Jones snapping out the question in a voice full of sharpness and challenge.

'Er, it's Cola,' said Jonathan.

'Poison! Bad for your system, rots your teeth. Throw it away.'

The words, and the haughty, biting way they'd been said, pushed Perry over the edge of his usual blandness into anger. 'Cut that out, Wally,' he said bluntly. 'As from now, cut it out. We're all equal here – we run our own lives. Leave the kid alone.'

Wally's eyes had swivelled to something else. 'Look at that!' she said, seeming breathless with shock. She pointed across the room to a loaf of pre-sliced bread. 'Pap!' she said furiously. 'Absolute pap ...'

Perry's anger raised itself another notch. 'Did you hear me?' he demanded, his voice hard and cold. 'I said cut it out. Now cut it out or the ...'

Still Wally was not to be stopped. 'You are what you eat you know,' she said. 'And we're not eating pap like that on the way to Mambay.'

That was enough for Peregrene. 'We're not going to Mambay,' he said grimly. 'The trip's off. Go home Mrs Jones, I'm busy.' He left the room.

Mrs Kidwallader Jones floundered out after him and down the stairs, followed by Roz and later by Charlie, whose shoulders were shaking with laughter. Jon stayed in the tower to man the radio. Nothing much seemed to be happening. An aircraft called for permission to overfly the field which he gave with a little glow of self-importance remembering to wish the pilot a polite 'Good Morning'. He sipped away at the Cola.

A full hour passed before Roz came back. 'My God, Jonny boy,' she said wearily. 'What a battle that's been. But we're on again. We're on for Mambay.'

Jonathan put his face close up to the window. 'She's leaving,' he said. 'She starting up the car.'

'Just as well. We can all cool off.'

'I hope she doesn't knock the tower down. Ah no, good, she's missed us. Blimey, she's the worst driver I've ever seen.'

'She's a sort of one-woman battering ram. You should have seen her wheedling round Perry. I've never seen him so tough with anyone before. He made her write a letter agreeing to do everything he says and giving him the right to pull out without notice. We can fly back at any time with or without her, and she's having to pay a thousand pounds in advance.'

'Blimey.'

'Jonathan.'

'Yes?'

'It, er, would be quite nice if you could find another word to use sometimes. You know, just occasion-ally.'

'Why? What's wrong with it?'

'Nothing. Here comes Perry. I bet he looks a bit battle scarred.'

As it turned out, Perry had a big, relaxed grin on his face when he wandered through the door. 'What a woman,' he said. 'She reminds me of Nero. She'll burn a few Christians in the morning. What about a coffee, Rozzie? Black and strong and hot.'

Roz laughed softly, showing her sparkling teeth and

21

looking marvellous. 'I think you need one. I'm going to enjoy this trip, Perry. My gosh, you're going to have your hands full with Wally. She might be the first woman I've ever met who's a match for you.'

'Yeah. Well, we'll see. If she's too much for me maybe Jonno can take the job over.'

'Blime ... Er, Crikey! No thanks. Anyway when do we go?'

'Tuesday. Take off nine o'clock. Get it cleared with your Mum if you're coming.'

'Of course I'm coming.'

'Okay. But get it cleared. And you'd better flight test Yankee Foxtrot with Charlie. Where is Charlie?'

'I'll find him.' Jonathan ran nimbly through the door and downstairs to look.

Charlie was at the workbench in the hangar doping a model aircraft, an impressive looking Super Sixty. Jonathan trotted up to him. 'Charlie,' he said, 'Perry says we've got to flight test Yankee Foxtrot. We're off to Mambay on Tuesday.'

'Come on then, mate. Let's go. You fly and I'll come along for the ride.' Jonathan picked up his two inflatable cushions and they strolled across to the old Aztec B, Golf Alpha Romeo Yankee Foxtrot. A change came over Charlie as they walked. The moodiness, the cynicism eased away to be replaced by a quiet alertness. Perry often said that Charlie was one of the best instructors in the aviation business, and you could see him changing into the role right now; the firm keen-eyed, top-class pilot in the man had taken charge.

'Do your DI first.' The daily inspection. Jonathan walked carefully round scanning the outside of Yankee Foxtrot for defects. The landing gear and tyres were good, wing surfaces clean, flaps and control surfaces

22

all okay. He opened the engine cowls and checked the oil. Everything looked right.

'I think she's fine. Shall we get in?'

'Has she flown today?' Charlie wasn't looking pleased.

'I don't think so. In fact no.'

'So?'

'So? Umm.'

'Come on, Jonno. You could have half a pint of water in the fuel, couldn't you? Drain it off.'

'Oh, crumbs! Yes.' He crouched under each wing and pressed the fuel drains open. Half a pint or so of fuel, very pungent to smell, splashed on to the grass at his feet. Then they clambered into the aircraft. 'You take the left-hand seat,' said Charlie.

The left-hand seat? The captain's place? That was something new, and Jonathan hesitated. 'Me? On the left?'

'Yep. I don't see why not. It's just as legal.'

'Blimey.' He settled in, arranged his cushions, one underneath and the other behind him, and fixed the seat belt.

'Let's get the clockwork running.' Charlie was leaving everything to him, and Jonathan began the drills. For a boy of 13½ he was pretty darned good with an aircraft by now – good enough to impress Charlie at times and that was saying a lot. He checked his brakes on, snapped the master switch to live, set the mixture control knobs to fully rich, primed the engines, selected fully fine pitch for both props, eased the throttles a quarter open, then pulled the starter toggle switch out and to the left. The left propeller began a slow, jerky rotation. In three seconds or so the Lycoming fired and, with a roar that never failed to thrill

Jonathan, the engine settled down to a 1,500 rpm warm-up. Moments later the starboard engine was blasting away too, and Yankee Foxtrot was aquiver with power.

Jonathan looked across at Charlie and smiled. It was obvious he was pleased with himself and with life. Charlie smiled back. The sound of a pair of well-tuned aero-engines running up did the same for these two as Beethoven does for the concert-going crowd.

They called for taxi clearance, rolled towards two-two and stopped into wind to run through the pre-take-off checks. 'Let's hear you call them out,' commanded Charlie, and Jonathan did so. Trim, Throttle friction, Mixture – fully rich and cold air – Pitch, Fuel turned on and booster pumps on, Flap, Gyros and Gauges okay, and Hatches and Harness secure.

'I'm all set. Shall I do the take-off?'

'You forgot something.'

Jonathan hated that. 'I did? What then?'

'Test for full and free movement of the controls. A stone might have jammed in somewhere when we taxied. It happens.'

'Crumbs, yes.' He pushed the control wheel fully forward and back, then tested all the way for aileron movement, both sides. The test was good.

'Let's go,' said Charlie.

Jonathan's heart began knocking up perhaps twice its normal beat rate as he eased the throttles smoothly forward and the Lycomings came on with their bellow-roar in fine pitch. His lips were tight and straight, every muscle in his body tense with the effort and con-centration. Yankee Foxtrot accelerated, thumping across the roughish grass, then the ride grew smoother as speed built up and two hundred yards before the boundary hedge, at the right moment exactly, Jonno eased the stick back and the heavy Aztec, after seeming to pause for a moment's thought, gently left the ground. As they flashed over the hedge, Captain Jonathan Kane reached down for the wheel-shaped lever and moved it to the gear-up position. Yankee Foxtrot settled her wheels into her belly and climbed steadily into a clear blue sky.

Charlie ran his eyes over the forty or so instruments and controls arrayed before them, approved of everything he saw and though he said nothing gave a little nod of his shaggy head. A clean take-off and an orderly climb.

Jonathan was on terrific form that day and everything just went right – even the landing approach and touch down. He did it all.

When they'd taxied back and snapped all the switches off, and the sudden silence settled round their ears – silence except for the gentle whine of the gyros running down – Charlie took Jonathan's knee in his big, left hand and shook it. 'That was all right, Captain,' he said. 'Not bad at all. Let's go.'

Chapter Two

SIR WILLIAM EXPLAINS

Jonathan biked home first thing on the Monday morning, persuaded his mother that he should be allowed to go to Mambay for a week, and did his packing. Shorts, red-trimmed underpants, a pair of ankle socks, open sandals and a couple of short-sleeved shirts were rammed into a haversack and then he was heading for the front door and yelling good-byes. Mrs Kane hurried towards him. 'My goodness,' she said, 'that was quick. Have you got everything you need?'

'Yes, Mum.'

'Toothpaste?'

'Well, no. But ...'

'Wait a minute.' She ran upstairs, got a new tube and pushed it into the haversack. 'Now, use it,' she said.

'Thanks.'

'Be careful.'

'Yes, yes.'

'And be careful what you eat.'

'Yes, Mum. Bye.'

'Good-bye darling,' she said and kissed him quickly on the cheek.

Jonathan pedalled energetically back, uphill a lot of the way, to Lonehead field. It was an pleasant, breezy morning. The windsock was sticking straight out like a huge, yellow finger when he got there. He parked his bike in the hangar and walked over to the ramshackle house where Peregrene lived in a curious mixture of comfort and disorder. No one was at home. They were all in the tower, Jon supposed. Puffing a bit, he climbed to the little attic bedroom, the room that was always his, and threw the haversack on the bed. From the window he could see the field, nearly all of it. Yankee Foxtrot had been rolled out of the hangar and Gerry Baines, the free-lance mechanic, was doing something to the starboard engine; all the cowls were off. Jonathan didn't much care for the look of that; he'd go over in a moment for a word with Gerry, get the news good or bad straight from the oracle.

He opened the little window and stood still for a moment enjoying the sight of the field spread out below him, and the suble scents of the country air. Simply being here, being with Perry and Charlie and Roz and the assorted collection of ageing aeroplanes, was truly the good life – all he could ever want was right here.

In a while he wandered out of the house and across towards the Aztec. Gerry was whistling cheerfully as he reassembled the cowls, his hands and wrists black with engine oil. 'It's just a loose wire,' he explained. 'I've fixed it. She can fly.'

That was a relief. Jonathan set off towards the hangar. Before he'd got halfway, a big black chauffeur-driven Cadillac rolled on to the field and stopped. A distinguished-looking man, tall and bespectacled, stepped out of the back. The man had quite a young-looking face but grey, almost white, hair that grew strongly and swept across his head like a thick capping of snow. He stood very straight, shoulders well back, and even his walk had something about it, an authority and grace. Jonathan studied him carefully from the

distance, decided to investigate and changed course
towards the car.

As he walked, Perry appeared from inside the han-
gar and got to the man first. The two men shook hands.
Jonathan moved quietly up and tagged on, listening.
The visitor threw a couple of quick looks at him, and
then Perry remembered to do some introducing.
'That's Jonathan,' he said briefly. 'One of the crew.
Jonno, we're having a visit here from Sir William
Krier.'

Sir William smiled, raised his hand in a little wave-
come-salute towards the boy and carried on talking.

'You see she does mean very well,' he was saying in a soft, cultivated tone of voice. 'She does the most extraordinary amount of good, but she is – what shall I say? – eccentric.'

'We've used some stronger words than that,' murmured Peregrene. 'Haven't we Jonno?'

'You bet.' You didn't need two guesses to know who they were on about.

'Well, I don't blame you. But I've come here to ask your co-operation. You see, I've looked into her fears that our supplies are not getting through, and it just isn't so. Yes, of course, there's a little thievery here and there – you'll always find a few wretches who'd steal from a blind beggar – but it's nothing significant. Nearly all the stuff is going through quite efficiently.'

'So you want to call the trip off?' A shadow flitted over Jonathan's expression at Peregrene's words. Then he brightened again.

'No. Not that. You know Mrs Kidwallader Jones! If she wants to do an investigation, she's going to do an investigation – come what may. No, what I'm asking you to do is to fly her there, keep her safe and fly her back as quickly as you can. She's going to have to be humoured, but I don't want anything to happen to her. Is that reasonable?'

'Why, sure. But as humouring goes it's kind of on the expensive side, isn't it?'

'Don't worry about that. It won't cost the fund a penny, and I won't let the lady herself pay either. I'm going to look after all that myself. It really is the only way. Nothing will stop her from going.'

'All right, Sir William. We'll get out there and get back again as fast as we can.'

'And safely!'

'Sure. And safely, too.'

'It might be wise not to mention this little talk we've had.'

'Yeah. I guess so.'

'Thanks.' The two shook hands, and Sir William, declining offers of a cup of coffee, climbed back into the Cadillac and sped quietly away.

Charlie appeared beside them as he went. 'Who's that lovely man?' he asked. 'Roz can't take her eyes off him – I think you're out.'

'That was Sir William Krier.'

'Oh yes? Up here about our old friend the Rock of Ages, eh?'

'Yeah.'

'What's he got to say?'

Perry explained over a cup of coffee in the tower. They agreed to aim for a three- or four-day trip, and to avoid telling Wally about Sir William's visit if that proved possible.

'I don't mind fooling around,' said Charlie. 'Not a bit. It's not my money. A nice trip out there and another one back. A bit of suntan on Wednesday, and some bright lights in the evening. A Mambay bottom or two to pinch too, maybe? That'll do me nicely.' He looked very pleased with himself and laughed.

'Charlie! D'you mind?' Roz was looking reproving. 'You're going to behave yourself out there, my lad. Remember you've got me coming along on the trip this time. And Mrs K.J. You'll be lucky if you see much of the bright lights, Charlie Thompson. Really lucky.' But Charlie went on chuckling and pulling his moustache.

Perry spent part of the day working out the flight plan for the long trip – just over twelve hundred nautical miles to Vanna, the little capital city of Mambay. He drew the intended track out carefully on his charts in a heavy black line.

Leave England at Worthing on airway Amber One cross channel, then down through central France for a possible landing at Limoges, but with Toulouse (quite a long way further south) filed as the 'alternate' – the airfield they could divert to; indeed, could and would divert to, all being well with the fuel tanks and weather. Then, after fuelling up, away again this time *en route* for Alicante on the Spanish coast, where they might or might not land, again depending on the tanks and weather conditions; and lastly the hundred and forty nautical mile hop across that great blue pond of a Mediterranean Sea to Mambay, the little state tucked neatly between the borders of Morocco and Algeria on the north coast of Africa – to the burning summer sun and a day or two of lazy pleasure.

The flight time worked out at eight hours three minutes. Perry was reckoning on nine all told, allowing for the Toulouse stop. That gave an arrival time of six in the evening. A good time, with the heat of the day waning fast.

'Where do we stay, Perry?' asked Jonathan. 'In a hotel or something?'

'I dunno. I guess so. We'll find somewhere to put our heads down.'

Then, during the afternoon, they learned where that 'somewhere' was to be – the royal palace, no less. Wally telephoned, booming through the earpiece at a pitch that made your ears twang and said she'd fixed it; they were all to be guests of the Sultan of Mambay.

She turned up in the NSU at about eight on Tuesday morning. Jonathan left the others finishing their breakfast and went out to meet the old girl. She'd just finished hauling herself out of the car and looked a bit flushed and hectic. 'Ah, there you are,' she said. 'I thought I might be late.'

'You've got heaps of time,' replied Jonathan. 'An hour.'

'You can get my bags out for me. I'm taking two.'

'What's that?' Jonathan was peering through the window of the car.

'My hat. I'll carry it.'

'Blimey. It needs an aeroplane all to itself.'

'It's to keep the sun off the back of my neck. Sun on your neck is bad you know.'

She lifted the hat out, a huge off-white affair with a brim about a foot wide. 'I don't want it sat on,' she added. Jonathan eyed the hat with a mixture of distaste and wonderment on his face, then dragged the bags out of the car.

'They're heavy enough,' he grumbled.

'Clothes and health foods, that's all. Come on.' She set off majestically towards the house using both hands to control the hat that had set up a gentle flapping movement in the morning breeze. Jonathan tottered along behind with the bags, muttering irritably.

They found the others clearing up the breakfast things. 'That's what I like to see,' beamed Mrs Kidwallader Jones. 'The men helping too.'

Roz smiled pleasantly. 'They generally do,' she said. 'And how are you this morning?'

'Fit. I'm always fit. There's never any need to be ill, you know.'

Charlie was looking at her strangely. 'You're a very wise woman, Mrs K.J.,' he said. 'I see you've brought your parachute.'

32

'That is my hat,' replied Wally coldly. 'I've had it nearly fifty years.'

'Really? Just fifty? It looks older. Ah well.' Charlie was baiting her already and enjoying it.

They had a difficult time getting ready for flight. They couldn't get both Wally's bags in the luggage compartment, so one had to go on the back seat. Then she nearly drove them crazy about the hat, until Perry firmly folded it up to a quarter size despite her protests and plonked it on the suitcase with her handbag on top to weight it down. Lastly, she couldn't stretch her leg up on to the wing to get into the aircraft and a five-minute struggle went on. In the end they got her through the door and right to the back of the aircraft, sitting beside her bag and hat. Jonathan sat in the middle row right, next to Roz, and Perry flew as Captain with Charlie co-piloting.

Gerry Baines, who was to run the airfield while they were away, came out to see the take-off and waved good-bye at six minutes past nine as Perry started up the engines. At eleven minutes past nine Yankee Foxtrot turned into wind and began the roaring acceleration across the grass, lifted off, zimmed over the hedge, tucked her landing gear away and set course on one-zero-six for Daventry and airway Amber One, the first part of the first leg of the long flight to Vanna Airport in Mambay.

This was the moment that did things for Jonathan, that never failed to set him glowing and tingling with suppressed excitement. Take-off with the Lycomings in full tumultuous sound, the ground falling away, the vastness of the sky ahead and Yankee Foxtrot looking beautiful with the sunshine on her wings. He had his headset on and plugged in. Leaning forward, he peered

between Perry's and Charlie's heads to scan the panel.
The needles were all in motion. Speed 104 knots, climb
rate eleven hundred feet a minute, manifold pressure
24 inches and twenty-four hundred rpm, the aircraft
already nicely settled down and as steady as Burton
town hall.

Charlie checked in by radio on one-three-five decimal two-five. 'London Airways. This is Aztec Golf Alpha Romeo Yankee Foxtrot out of Lonehead at one-one climbing to flight level seven zero estimating Daventry two-eight.'

The controller came briskly back. 'Romeo Yankee Foxtrot, good morning. You are cleared to join Amber One at Daventry.'

Charlie acknowledged briefly and they levelled out at 7,000 feet. The world looked small from there, small and different.

Jonathan settled back contently in his seat to enjoy the good life of a flying man. Then a finger jabbed him on the shoulder and he looked round to see Mrs Kidwallader Jones leaning forward so close that their noses almost touched. 'Where are we?' she asked loudly.

'Well, blimey – we've only just started,' said Jonathan.

'I want a map.'

'What for?'

'I like to know where I'm going. Find me a map.'

Roz turned round helpfully. 'If I were you I'd just leave it to them,' she said. She had to speak loudly to be heard above the engines.

'Well, you're not me and I want a map.' The friendly smile Roz had been showing cooled a bit and she glanced questioningly at Jonno, who swivelled his microphone into place and spoke on the intercom to Charlie.

'The silly old trout wants a map. Can we give her one?'

Charlie half turned his head. 'She couldn't read it,' he said. 'Tell her to go to sleep.'

'You tell her.'

Charlie fumbled about with his right hand, then silently handed back a pilot's map. Jonathan passed it on to the back.

Soon she had the thing unfolded and spread out all over the back like a blanket. Jonathan could sense the mounting confusion behind him. 'This is a very funny map,' shouted Wally at last. 'Haven't you got a better one?'

Jonathan swung the mike out of the way and hollered back at her. 'It's a pilot's map. It's what we always use.'

'I'd rather have an ordinary road map.'

'We don't have one. We don't generally go by road in the Aztec.' Jonathan felt pleased with that remark and he could tell that Charlie had heard it too and was chuckling to himself.

For a minute Wally had nothing more to say then, suddenly, she bundled the map up and thrust it forward on to Jonathan's lap. 'It's no good to me,' she said. 'A stupid sort of map. You can fold it up and give it back.'

'Thank you!' yelled Jonathan sarcastically. 'Thank you *very* much.' He refolded the crumpled map and balanced it on his knee.

Perry had been very quiet. He usually was in the air. He didn't like unnecessary chat and had a way of turning his cool grey eyes on passengers who wagged too much until the words seemed to stick in the roofs of their mouths. His soft, sleepy voice with its hint of the northern states where he'd been raised, came through the intercom now to Charlie. 'Report us in at Midhurst,' he said.

'Okay.'

Charlie watched the VOR dial intently and soon

the little 'To' flag disappeared and, after a pause, the 'From' flag came up. Charlie pressed the transmit button and reported they were overhead at Midhurst beacon. London Airways acknowledged briefly and Perry changed course to one-five-one for Worthing. They flew on, the Lycomings pulling smoothly and sounding good. Perry took his hands off the stick and made a little gesture towards Charlie, who put his own big hands on and did the flying for a while. Yankee Foxtrot's auto-pilot never worked and so pilotage was done the hard way – all of it by hands and feet. Perry reckoned it was the right way to fly anyway. 'Keeps you awake, and wakeful pilots stay alive.'

At eight minutes past ten they flew over Worthing and Perry checked in on radio. A new little flurry of excitement gathered inside Jonathan as he looked down on the seaside town with its pier and red fun-nelled ships and the grey-looking ocean they were start-to cross. The coastline disappeared behind. They were still on Amber One steering one-five-one – south-east for France, Spain and the distant Mambay.

They tuned in to the French controller and re-ported, using the standard, terse message pattern: where they were, the time in minutes past the hour (eleven minutes past four, for instance, coming over as a cryptic 'one-one'), their height and their estimated time at the next reporting point.

The French controller spoke immaculate English with a sexy Paris accent that always amused Jonathan and pleased him. For one thing, it showed they were getting somewhere. 'Yank-*ee* Fogstrot. Paris Airways. Advise Mantes.'

The Mantes beacon came up at five-seven and Pere-grene duly advised. They changed airways to Red

Ten, steering one-nine-five, everything still going well.

It occurred to Jonathan that Wally had been un-usually quiet and he turned round to have a look at her. She had an odd expression on her face: eyes closed, but not quite fully, so that some of the whites still showed, and mouth sagging open. 'What a sight!' he said to Roz, speaking loudly against the engine noise and pointing backwards. 'The old trout's asleep.'

The pudgy finger jabbed him in the shoulder again. 'I am *not* asleep,' she said, 'and don't you dare call me names.'

Jonathan reddened. 'Sorry,' he mumbled. 'I thought you—'

'I *know* what you thought. It just so happens my mind was at rest on a higher plane. I can do it at will. I call it wakesleep. An hour of wakesleep does me as much good as an hour or ordinary sleep does most people, but I'm alert all the time. Don't miss a thing – not a thing.' She settled back, opened her mouth, rolled her eyeballs upwards and went instantly back to her higher plane.

Out beyond the left window of Yankee Foxtrot was the panorama of Paris. Looming out of it all, gaunt and unmistakable, was the Eiffel Tower. Jonathan leaned across, close to Roz to look out at the view. She was enjoying the sight too.

They flew on through almost clear skies, chasing southwards after the sun. A Pan Am Boeing passed above them, much higher, travelling north on Red Ten.

At Chateaudun they reported in again and changed course to two-zero-four for Amboise, still on the airway. Charlie turned to Peregrene. 'Let's give 'em a call for the divert,' he said.

'Yeah.' Perry had a good look round the cockpit, checked fuel, temperatures and pressures, then called Paris. 'Paris Airways. Lima Yankee Foxtrot. Request permission to route to our alternate, Toulouse.'

Back came the Paris controller. 'Yank-*ee* Fogstrot. Stand by.'

Soon after, Paris called again. 'Yank-*ee* Fogstrot, Paris Airways. What fuel have you?'

'Yankee Foxtrot. We have a further two hours and ten minutes endurance on passing Limoges. Forward estimate for Toulouse one-two five-five. Will have forty-seven usable at Limoges.'

'Yank-*ee* Fogstrot. You are cleared to Toulouse. Join Amber Three-Four at Amboise.'

Charlie twisted round to see Jonno and Roz. He was looking pleased and relaxed. 'We're okay for Toulouse,' he said. 'That's good. You okay, Jonno?'

'Yes thanks. Fine.'

Charlie gestured towards the rear. 'What's happened to her? Drunk or something?'

A rush of discretion came to Jonathan. He pulled the mike near to his mouth and almost whispered his reply on intercom. 'It's what she calls wakesleep,' he explained. 'She hears everything.'

They arrived at Toulouse exactly on time having won back the eleven minutes lost at the start of the flight. Perry put Yankee Foxtrot down at three minutes to one on runway one-five. A super landing, so gently done you hardly knew when the moment of contact happened, and they taxied clear to the parking area. Charlie pulled the mixture controls to fully lean. The Lycomings stopped abruptly, and suddenly the world seemed a quiet place.

Jonathan looked apprehensively round at Wally.

She was evidently still at rest on her higher plane. 'We're here Mrs Kid ... I mean, Wally,' he said helpfully.

She opened her eyes and closed her mouth. 'Here? Where is here?' she asked.

'Toulouse.'

'Ah, Toulouse. I hope it has a lavatory.'

They had another struggle getting her through the door and down off the wing. Charlie got her on to the ground in the end by wrapping his strong arms round her and lifting her down like a sack of beans.

'Come on everyone, let's go eat,' said Perry.

Fifty minutes later, refuelled to the brim, Yankee Foxtrot was cleared for take-off. Jonathan had talked his way into the co-pilot's seat and made the radio call. 'All right, Jonno,' murmured Perry through the intercom. 'Let's go.' He pushed the throttles forward and the Lycomings got down to it again, roaring away on full power.

'Gear up,' said Perry at a hundred feet, and Jonno reached for the safety gate, slid it aside and pulled the wheel-shaped knob up. Then Perry spoke again. 'You have control,' he said, and took his hands and feet off.

'Okay, I have her.' Jonathan took the wheel in his neat hands, holding it gently but firmly, a subtle pressure of the fingers that let 'feel' come through from the aircraft, to fly with economy of movement and always with precision – that was the aim. He put his feet lightly on the rudder pedals and took a quick look at the panel. A hundred and five knots, one-five-two degrees. He felt a little tense; it was always like that just at first, at the start of the tricky task of flying well enough for Perry. Peregrene Langhorne, master pilot, the one-time boy who flew his first solo at fifteen ('they thought I was a little bit older,' he would explain as an aside) and survived his first crash at sixteen – into power lines while crop spraying – forgave nothing careless in the air. You flew well or you got the hell out of the seat.

'Hold two-seven-zero for Point Charlie,' said Peregrene. 'One five-five knots at flight level eight-five.'

'Two-seven-zero,' repeated Jonathan starting a climbing turn, right, on to course. As they passed through 3,000 feet, Perry adjusted the altimeters to the internationally agreed standard setting of one-zero-one-three point two on the millibar scale. Jonno nodded his thanks and continued the climb. At 8,500 feet he trimmed for level flight, eased the throttles for 155 knots and got everything settled down.

Perry was watching without seeming to, using that extraordinary knack of sideways vision he had, his corner-of-the-eye range. He had a word now on the intercom with Charlie. 'We've got the Pyrenees just ahead,' he said. 'We'll be going on up to twelve and a half thousand. Get everybody organized with oxygen. Have a special look at Wally. We don't want her turning blue.'

'Yeah. Okay. Yeah, yeah. Hell!' Charlie turned round slowly, like a reluctant soldier advancing to battle and was relieved to see Wally looking as normal as she ever did, and awake. 'Look here,' he boomed at her, scowling. 'We're going above oxygen height to cross the mountains, put this over your gob.' He clamped a little, portable oxygen cylinder and mouthpiece to her face. 'And press this button. Go on, try it.'

She removed it at once, pushing his hand away.

'Nobody told me about this,' she said tartly. 'What is it?'

'I'm telling you now. It's oxygen. Try it.'

The old girl was all indignation and suspicion. 'I don't care for this sort of thing,' she said. 'I don't like breathing in *chemicals*.'

'Oh, for God's sake! Will you just do as you're told for once?' Charlie was flaring up now and looming towards her over the seat. 'It's only oxygen, pure, pure oxygen. You breathe it all the time in the air. Now, just put it up to your silly mouth and try it!'

'Don't shout at me,' retorted Wally, 'you rude, vulgar man.' Then slowly she put the mask to her face and pressed the button.

Roz squeezed her hand. 'That's it, Wally,' she said. 'Well done.'

Perry glanced across at Jonathan and winked. Jonno smiled broadly showing his trim, white teeth, and screwing up his eyes. He put a hand over the microphone. 'Poor old Charlie,' he said. 'Rather him than me.'

'Yeah, well, he's bigger than you. Okay, let's start the climb. Full throttle – that'll give twenty-two or twenty-three inches manifold pressure – and let's have twenty-four hundred revs. Level at twelve-thousand five-hundred.' As Jonno moved the pitch and throttle levers for climbing power, Perry turned round and shouted the oxygen instructions to them all. 'At ten thousand feet I'll give you a call and I want everyone on oxygen then,' he said. 'Hold the mouthpiece firmly to your face and keep the button pressed. I'll give you another shout when we're low enough to put the stuff away again. Keep an eye on each other. If you see anyone acting strangely, it means there's something wrong with the supply – tell me about it. Is everyone clear on that?'

They crossed the high peaks of the Pyrenees with the oxygen on, in silence — silence except for the throb and roar of the hard-worked Lycomings. One very high peak still had its capping of midsummer snow and seemed strangely close to Yankee Foxtrot's belly. The sun still shone, and the mountain shadows seemed very dark.

The oxygen phase didn't last long. Twenty-five minutes out from Toulouse, Perry reached over and throttled the engines back for the start of the let down. At ten thousand feet the oxygen masks all came off and normality returned. They came on down to flight level seven five and at three o'clock passed over Zaragoza, set in the broad valley beyond the mountains.

Perry called Barcelona FIR for clearance via Alicante direct to Mambay. The last stage of the flight would be 140 nautical miles across the Med to the North African coast.

'We should have twenty-three gallons usable reserves Charlie,' he said. 'That's enough.'

Charlie leaned over Jonathan's shoulder to study the fuel gauges. 'Yeah,' he said. 'Everything's going for us this time. Let's drive all the way.'

As he settled back in his seat, Wally jabbed him, three powerful little pressures with her stubby finger. 'What's the matter?' she asked.

'The matter?'

'Yes. What were you talking about just now?'

Charlie tugged away at the right side of his moustache for a moment before replying. 'The weather,' he said at last. 'We were just remarking what a lovely day it is. Get your hat ready. We're almost there.'

Perry and Jon took it in turns to fly, doing stints of about an hour each. Yankee Foxtrot was steaming along beautifully, and when Perry had control Jonno would spend long, contented minutes, his chin cupped in his hand, gazing through the window at the big Lycoming doing its stuff out there on the wing. An aero-engine looks so inactive. He pondered about that. Hard to imagine the heavy pistons flashing up and down, the hot gases, the hammering tappets, the high pressures and stresses going on as twelve gallons of aviation spirit an hour were sucked into the cylinders and burnt. Well, there was plenty of noise to show what was going on.

They crossed the coast and soon afterwards Perry gave control back to Jonathan. 'Steer two-one-zero,' he said. 'A hundred and forty to go for Vanna Airport. Are you okay?'

'Yes, fine.' Jonathan wriggled into an easier position on the cushions.

'Not tired?'

'Well, not specially.'

'Hold her where she is then. I'll call Vanna soon.'

They flew on without more talk, across the long blueness of the Mediterranean Sea. Roz had nodded off, and Wally seemed to be wakesleeping her way to the higher planes again with her eye-whites showing and mouth oddly slack. Charlie remained alert, hunching forward from time to time to read the panel. Twice he rumpled Jonathan's hair playfully from behind, and each time the boy acknowledged, lifting his left hand, a slow slight movement, fingers extended, then placing it back on the wheel; a silent exchange of regard between friends.

Thirty minutes flying time from Vanna, Peregrene tried a transmission on one-one-nine decimal seven. 'Vanna. Aztec Golf Romeo Yankee Foxtrot. Do you read me?' He released the button and waited, then pressed it and tried again. 'Vanna. Aztec Golf Alpha Romeo Yankee Foxtrot. Do you read?' Another pause. He turned to Jonathan. 'How about that then, Jonno?'

Jonathan shrugged. 'Maybe they've all gone home,' he suggested.

But seconds later, just as Perry was about to repeat the call, the mush of transmitter static came through the earphones, and Perry raised an expectant finger, waiting.

'Yangee Fogs. Vanna approach. Redding you tree. Ovair.'

Perry brightened. 'Vanna. Yankee Foxtrot. Strength three also. Estimating arrival five-five.'

They were cleared to reduce height to five thousand on the local QNH for a straight-in approach and landing on runway two-eight.

'They sound French,' said Jonathan when the radio chatter finished.

'Yep. They speak a lot of French. It's their second language.'

'Blimey. Everyone seems French these days.'

'Wally says they speak English, too. Clever, eh?'

Now Charlie leaned forward again. 'Just as flippin' well they do,' he said. 'I never could get on with French.' A moment later Peregrene took control. 'I guess you're a bit tired, Jonno,' he said. 'I think I'd better put her down.'

Jonathan did feel tired; not impossibly so, but tired enough to be glad he didn't have to sweat it out on the final approach. He took his hands and feet off, folded his arms and contentedly sat back to watch Peregrene begin his usual faultless performance.

The last bit of the approach took them low over the

45

sea. Jonathan glanced down at the rolling waves as Yankee Foxtrot flashed across them, gear and flaps down and straining for the runway.

A strip of sand went blurrily by, and a square of scrub, and then the wheels were skimming over a batch of unlit approach lights, and moments later were touching gently down on the runway.

The controller directed them to a parking apron near the little HQ, a building of aluminium and glass that glittered brightly in the early evening sun. Perry turned Yankee Foxtrot into wind, locked the brakes on and pulled the mixture control levers to fully lean. The Lycomings shut abruptly down. He turned all switches off and hung his headset on the control wheel. 'Ladies and gentlemen,' he said in that drawly voice of his – that misleadingly sleepy low-key voice – 'we've made it. You are now in the North African town of Vanna. Jonathan, let's get out of this goddam airplane and stretch our legs.'

Jonathan moved nimbly on to the wing, then hopped to the ground, followed by Perry and Roz. Charlie waited by the door for Wally. 'Come on then, you poor old soul,' he said, but she took ages to get out of the backseat. When she did make it to the door she handed him her huge hat. 'Kindly take that for me,' she said, 'and then get my bag out, please. And handle my things carefully.'

Charlie looked at the ridiculous hat in silence, then stuck it on his own hairy head and squeezed past Wally, who was backing slowly out through the door. He clambered down to the ground and turned back to see how the old girl was getting on. She'd got a foot too far out along the wing.

'Keep your ruddy feet on the walkway – on the black bit!' yelled Charlie.

'The silly thing isn't wide enough,' she retorted, easing her way towards the trailing edge of the wing.

'It's not built for people your shape. Hurry up.'

Wally stood there, holding on to a little handle, and quaked with anger. 'I'll . . . I'll report you to someone if you go on speaking to me like that,' she said. 'Kindly remember I am the client.'

'Get a move on then, Client.' He grabbed her waist in the same bearhug he'd used at Toulouse and breathing hard heaved her down on to the ground.

A uniformed man wearing polished boots and with a heavy pistol slung round his middle was striding towards them. As they all met, he saluted. 'Madame Kidwallader Jones?' he said inquiringly.

Wally stepped forward looking happier now, and consciously important. '*I* am Mrs Kidwallader Jones,' she said.

'Ah. Bon jour, Madame. I have instructions from His Majesty, King Abdellah, to greet you. Welcome to Mambay.'

Wally beamed. 'There now,' she said. 'How charming of the King. How sweet of him. Er, thank you.'

The uniformed man bowed. 'I am Colonel Sidi Moukef. I am entirely at your service, madame.'

'Well, that *is* nice.'

The Colonel's eyes had moved now to Peregrene and Charlie. 'One of you will be Mr Langhorne?' he suggested.

Peregrene stepped forward. 'That's me, Colonel,' he said, and they shook hands. Then Perry introduced the others.

From nowhere three men appeared to help unload and carry the bags through the airport building to a waiting nine-seater minibus and bearded driver. The Colonel helped them in, putting Wally at the front, and beckoned the driver to start. He explained he would be following them to the palace in his military car.

They travelled quite fast, and Jonathan tried to take it all in, the fascination of Africa – the veiled women, ferocious-looking men, red stone windowless buildings, red soil, a red river even, camels, donkeys with enormous loads on their backs, exotic trees and the huge subtropical sun already quite low in the sky. And all the time, to remind him of realities, Wally was bouncing about on the front seat like a beach ball – a tiresomely talkative beach ball with opinions, mostly critical ones, on everything. Jonno felt better when he realized that the driver wasn't understanding a word she said.

They turned in through the palace gates and were immediately stopped by sentries. Then, after the Colonel had drawn up behind them and shouted instructions in Arabic, the sentries stepped back and waved them through. They sped on down a short, tree-lined approach road.

They drew up at a long outer wall, perhaps 30 feet high, red again and unrelieved by windows but with gilded gates set centrally. Through the gates you could see a colourfully tiled courtyard, and, beyond that, the palace building, a two-storey symmetrical block with twin cupola-topped towers placed towards the rear and rising fully 60 feet. Four sentries stood on guard, two by the outer gates and two at the back of the courtyard by the royal front door.

The Colonel led them out of the minibus and through the courtyard to the palace entrance. To Jonathan's surprise at the door he pulled an old-fashioned bell string, then cocked his head, listening for the jangling sound that duly jangled in the distance. It didn't seem very royal. Where were the trumpets, the heralds, the marching soldiers – all the trappings of palace life? Even the sentries, in ill-fitting khaki uniforms, seemed half asleep.

An immense, thickly bearded man appeared at the door. He was wearing the traditional Arabian burnous; it reminded Jonathan of a beach-robe – a one-piece, striped, cotton garment with a hood (for the moment hanging limply down at the back) and with big, slack sleeves. Round his waist the man wore a wide scarlet sash with a bone-handled dagger stuck behind it.

He and the Colonel talked for a while in Arabic. In a few moments the Colonel turned to them all and explained that he was leaving now. 'This is Benahid,' he explained. 'The King's principal servant and body-guard. He will look after you well. I expect to join you for dinner this evening. *Au revoir.*' He saluted and turned away.

'Please enter the King's palace,' said Benahid, opening the door wide. He led them through a lobby, then across a broad mosaic-floored hall and up stairs that had no handrail to their bedrooms, a separate room for each person. A watchful servant sat in the corridor and looked like a permanent fixture, faintly menacing in his silence. Other servants brought their bags, and they were left to rest for a little while. At seven, Benahid had explained, the King wished to receive them in his private suite.

The room was hot. Jonathan took off his jeans, pulled on a pair of lightweight blue shorts and sprawled wearily on to his bed, grateful for half an hour or so of peace. He glanced about him. It was all very different, very eastern. A low bed, more mosaic flooring – cold and polished but softened by a white and purple rug – narrow windows, a high ceiling, colourfully patterned walls, a glass chandelier. He closed his eyes. Yes, he was tired. Lonehead field seemed a million miles away – more – a world away.

When he opened his eyes again Charlie's hairy face was grinning down at him. 'Come on, Captain,' he was saying. 'Wakey wakey. You're required downstairs. And by royal command. Let's go.'

Chapter Three

STRAINING FOR SPEED

On the way down to the King, Wally babbled some advice to the rest of them. 'They do things differently here,' she explained. 'You'll probably have to eat with your fingers, and from the same dish. Don't pick and choose — just eat whatever's right in front of you. And you must eat something from every dish. They call it honouring the food. It doesn't make any difference whether you like it or not. D'you all understand that? Just eat.'

'Blimey,' said Jonathan feelingly.

'And there'll be mint tea to drink, too. You must drink *two* cups of it. It's very rude not to.'

'Cods!' muttered Charlie.

Roz looked at him sharply. 'Charlie, you've got to behave yourself this time,' she said. 'Our host is a King after all.'

'Well,' said Peregrene blandly, 'if he doesn't do things right the King can always have his head cut off. One good swing of a sabre should do it.'

Wally didn't smile. Aglow with importance, she was slightly ahead of the others, the leader, strutting along and tucked closely in behind the vast figure of Benahid.

King Abdellah was seated on a low, brocaded cushion when they entered his private sitting room. Wally rushed towards him in a flurry of excitement. 'Ah, ah,

Your Majesty!' she gushed. 'Your Royal Majesty. I'm Mrs Kidwallader Jones of Save Mambay. What an honour and pleasure.' She gave a little bob of a bow.

The King nodded his head. 'I hope you've had a pleasant journey,' he said mildly. 'Please present your friends.'

Roz came first and had quite an effect on the King. Smilingly, he took her hand in his. 'Nom de Dieu,' he said. 'You have great beauty, Rosemary-Anne. Rose! La fleur, eh? Sit here, beside me.' He pulled her gently down towards a cushion on his right and Roz, looking cool and demure in a simple, white cocktail dress settled very close to him. Wally's head began to jerk again as she carried on with the introductions.

Jonathan came last and was also specially warmly greeted. 'Aha!' said the King shaking his hands. 'A little English boy – c'est très, très bon. You are strong Jonathan, a warrior – I think so. I was once like you. Can you fight with a sword?'

'Er, I've never really tried,' said Jonathan lamely.

'And ride a stallion?'

'I ... I don't think so.'

The King laughed. 'Then I will teach you,' he said. 'Sit here.' As Jonathan settled nimbly down on the King's left, Wally's jerking rate visibly increased.

'Please, all of you, be seated,' the King said, gesturing towards other cushions on the floor. Peregrene and Charlie settled down on theirs, but Wally was immediately in trouble. She stood, eyeing the distance down to the cushion beside her, breathing hard. Then, quickly, Benahid appeared beside her and gently helped her down. As soon as they were settled the mint tea came round, poured by Benahid from a silver teapot with a high, elegant spout.

Charlie put his nose inside his cup and sniffed suspiciously. The King smiled benevolently on them all, then raised his cup. 'God be with you,' he said, and drank.

Wally saw a chance for leadership again. 'To Your Majesty's health and long life,' she said grandly, swallowing an ample mouthful. The others sipped tentatively at the hot, light green liquid, expecting it to be worse than it was. By about the third sip, Jonathan quite liked the stuff – an odd mixture of flavours, sweetness with peppermint, and not bad when you'd tuned in. The cups were small and of very fine, almost transparent china. Roz had a brief fit of giggles watching Charlie whose ragged moustache hung down the outside of his cup like hay overflowing a farmcart. He looked very gloomy and on edge.

Wally had another go at leadership. 'Well now, Your Majesty,' she said. 'Of course you know why we're – ah, I am here?'

The King seemed not to have heard. 'I hope you all enjoy your stay in Mambay,' he murmured. 'You may find the weather rather hot. But whatever you wish that it is in my power to give, I will gladly give you. Ask and it shall be done.'

Confusion showed on Wally's face. She'd blundered off a bit too quickly and knew it; hadn't waited for the ceremonial pleasantries. She battled on: 'Your Majesty is most kind,' she said, forcing a little smile that could have been shaped round an acorn. 'Most kind; most graciously kind. I speak for us all when I say what a pleasure it is to be here in your palace. Ahem. One just regrets being here for the reason that we are; such a sombre occasion.'

That was better. She could see from the King's face

that she was doing much better now. She raised her cup a second time. 'May fortune soon smile again on Mambay,' she said resonantly and nodded at Peregrene.

'Oh, yeah, sure,' said Perry raising his cup too and joining her in the toast. 'We'll all drink to that.' And they all did.

The King seemed ready to talk now. 'What do you plan to do here, Mrs Kidwallader Jones?' he asked.

'Your Majesty.' She uttered the words with heavy emphasis and leaned forward awkwardly, confidentially. 'Your Majesty, since the droughts came to Mambay and your people began to suffer we have shipped great quantities of supplies out here – blankets, food, medical supplies, all that – but I believe things are going wrong. I know Your Majesty will regret this as much as I do,' she lowered her eyes, 'but I think the supplies are being stolen. I have come here to find out the truth.'

A tired look came over the King's face. 'That won't take long,' he said.

'Won't, uh, take long?' Wally lost a little of her swing again.

The King pointed towards the rear of the large room. 'You see those stairs?' he asked. 'Well, climb them, climb right to the top of the tower. Look out of the window and tell me what you see.'

An awkward silence fell, caused as much by the King's expression as by his words, and then Perry stood up. 'Come on,' he said. 'Let's take a look.' He held a hand out to Wally and hauled her to her feet.

It took a long time to reach the top. Jonno had nipped up ahead and was waiting on the top floor. 'There's nothing much to see,' he shouted. 'Just some beaten-up lorries.'

They made it up the last few steps to join him at last and gathered round a cluster of unglazed windows. Vanna lay spread out below them. Already dusk was settling in and the streets were quiet. But there, in the broad Avenue Mimoun, behind the palace, was a line-up of old-fashioned lorries. There were four, all ten-wheelers.

Peregrene spelled it out. 'There go your latest food supplies, Wally,' he said. 'I think they're just about to leave town.'

When they had got downstairs again, the King was standing over by the window, looking out across the royal gardens to the west.

Wally hurried up to him. 'Your *Majesty*!' she said. 'What's in those lorries?'

The King turned to face her. 'Your supplies, of course. They'll be away tonight, all those lorries. Yes, across the border and away.'

'But, but ... Your Majesty. I – I don't understand. You mean you *know* about this? You *know*? And people are *starving*?' Wally's indignation was genuine and on the whole impressive.

'I regret it,' said the King quietly. 'I regret it very much.'

'Then do something – stop it! You're the King.' She was going too fast again, and again she knew it. The King, a slightly built, thin-faced man of middle age was turning to confront her indignation and there was the glitter of royal anger in his eye. 'Oh Your Majesty, I don't mean to be rude,' Wally babbled on, 'but I beg you to explain.' She wrung her hands and shook with anguish.

The King pointed to some low, divan-type seating covered in gaily striped materials. 'Let us sit over there,' he said, 'and before long we will eat. First I will tell you what has happened.'

King Abdellah made a slow start and while he sat in the corner formed by two divans lost in what seemed to be deep and troubled thoughts, Benahid brought round the second cup of mint tea.

He began at last. 'In the name of Allah I'll tell you the truth,' he said. 'It's a painful truth, and I am a deeply troubled man, but I'll hold nothing back.

'Nineteen years ago I married my second wife, Fatima. She was very beautiful! My little pearl I called her. My pearl! Well, yes, I think perhaps the word was apt, for pearls are cold and hard as well as beautiful, and she was that – cold and hard, so very hard. She was only sixteen, yet she obsessed, possessed me. It was extraordinary. Me, a King. Whatever Fatima wished me to do for her, I did.

'And Fatima wished power for her brother, Youssef Fetouaki. In time I put him in charge of my army. And in more time, he took my army from me.'

A lengthy silence followed while the King gazed absently into his almost empty cup. Then he straightened himself and looked round at them all, one by one. 'The truth is,' he said at last, 'I am a King in name only. A King without power, without wives. I am nothing – a puppet. Youssef and Fatima rule Mambay today. I have been a fool.'

Jonathan was surprised to feel himself redden with embarrassment as another agony of silence settled in the room. Then Roz broke it, gently. 'Perhaps you have just been too trusting, Your Majesty,' she said.

The King smiled across at her, a sudden warmth coming into his bleak expression. 'Thank you my dear, that is kind,' he said. The tension eased and

Jonathan returned to his normal colour. It was hard to think of this tired-looking man as a warrior — fighting with swords, riding stallions. Well, of course, that had been long ago, and things had changed.

Wally seemed to be puffing up with excitement and about to speak, but Perry got in first.

'Sir,' he said. 'You seem to have big problems here. Too big, I guess, for us to help with. I'd like your permission to fly out of Vanna tomorrow morning. We'll take off at nine.'

'We will do no such think.' Wally had the floor now.

Perry looked across at the old girl levelly, at the heaving breasts and furious eyes. 'I'm in charge of the airplane,' he said. 'If I say we go, we go.'

'Not at all. By no means. You can say that *you* go — certainly. But nobody says when *I* go, except me, and I've got some investigating to do before I leave Mambay. I am *not* flying out tomorrow morning.'

'Jeeze. Now look, Wally . . .'

'I am not leaving until I'm ready.'

'Go on,' said Charlie, looking quite amused for the moment, 'admit it, Perry. You're beaten.'

'Let us eat,' suggested the King, and clapped his hands. Benahid appeared. 'Is Colonel Moukef here?' the King asked.'

'Yes, Your Majesty.'

'Show him in, then serve the meal.'

Benahid bowed himself out, returning a minute later with the Colonel, who greeted them all with grave politeness and sat down. Suddenly, the main doors to the King's apartment opened and four servants struggled in carrying a table already laid with fine silver dishes of steaming food. The table was brought over and set down before the King and his party. Benahid came round with perfumed water which he poured on the fingers of each person's right hand. Then the King put his fingers into a huge round dishful of meat and maize and dried fruits, and the meal began. Jonathan approached the dish with extreme suspicion, but saw the pebble eyes observing him and decided he'd better honour the wretched thing as ordered. It turned out to be very good and made him realize his hunger. He ate eagerly and so did the others. Even Wally, for all her emotion, was ploughing into the steaming dish with her little, ring-clad fingers and going well.

When they finished there was still some left, but full honour had certainly been done. They rinsed their fingers in silver bowls of water, and then, slowly, carefully and with a strange expression in his eyes, King Abdellah picked up an orange, peeled it and handed it to Roz. 'Le fruit de l'amitié,' he said, smiling. 'The fruit of friendship, eh?' Roz, aware that there was something old and important about this gesture, thanked him politely and ate the orange while the King looked on indulgently.

Wally was watching too, and another little burst of the headshakes showed that something was going on in her mind. She'd been unusually quiet while the main part of the eating was going on, but now she opened up with some verbal gunfire.

'Your Majesty,' she said. 'We're going to put Mambay right! Yes, put Mambay right. It can be done you know. Everything can be done if the will is there. First we must deal with Youssef and get the people fed. Then you must modernize the way of life here ...'

Charlie had heard enough already, and his feeling showed. The old girl was out of her tree again. Deal with Youssef. *Deal* with him – and get the people fed, just like that. 'You deal with Youssef,' he said sarcastically, glowering across the table. 'Tell him to stand in the corner.'

Wally's sharp little eyes turned to wilt him, which they wholly failed to do. 'I certainly shall deal with Youssef,' she retorted. 'I'll gather the facts and present them to Sir William Krier. Then we'll turn world opinion on the dreadful things this Youssef's doing. That'll see *him* out of the way. Remember, I'm not afraid of *any* man.' She focused on the King again and prepared to come back to her theme. Perry nudged Charlie with his elbow. 'Go on, Charlie,' he said, 'admit it. You're beaten.'

'Cods!' muttered Charlie, ripping into an orange with his big red hands.

'As I was saying, Your Majesty,' Wally was going well now, really well, like a Spanish galleon in a force five wind, 'you must modernize your way of life. Let me be your adviser. For a start you must unveil your women, set the poor things free. Tell me, Your Majesty,' she lowered her voice now and looked suddenly coy and secretive, 'tell me, are there still such things as, as groups of, er, kept women here? Such things as, you know, harems?'

The King's expression had gone rather cold again. 'Are there harems in Mambay?' he repeated. 'Is the sun still in the sky?'

It took Wally a moment to decide how to deal with so oblique a reply. Then she was away again. 'Well, all that must stop – it's disgraceful. No more veils, no more harems. Mambay women must be free.' The last words were said with such emotion they were almost sung, like part of a national anthem.

The cold look on the King's face had gone colder

still, and Jonathan's interest grew; a bit of a punch-up seemed to be coming.

'You mean we should copy the ways of Europe and the west?' asked the King. 'Everyone is happy there? The women do not complain? There is no unrest? No violence, crime, suicide? Hah, I read the foreign papers, Mrs Kidwallader Jones. I know about your ways. Your mess is worse than ours, and I know about Russia too, and their ways. Their mess is worse than yours, much worse than yours; and yours much worse than ours. You can be sure of nothing.'

Perry spoke, and did so softly, coolly as usual. 'Sir,' he said. 'It's *your* people who are starving.'

For a second or two the King was silent, then nodded his head in acknowledgement. 'Some of my people are hungry,' he agreed. 'That is true. It is also unusual, and it should not be.' He seemed close to despair.

'Set the women free,' begged Wally again, loudly, 'banish their veils, Your Majesty – banish their veils.'

Charlie had had enough of her single-mindedness by now. 'Wrap it up,' he snapped. 'For God's sake stop raving on about women and veils. The people here are starving.'

King Abdellah raised his thin hands for silence. 'Do you read much, Mrs Kidwallader Jones?' he asked. 'No, no, I expect you haven't the time. Most people haven't the time these days. But I do have time and I read a lot. I commend you to the writings of a modern American, Robert Ardrey – a great student of mankind. Read his books and marvel at the way we all misread our nature. Men must continue to be the hunters and liberated women are not, I think, the happiest.' He looked across at Jonno. 'Do I make any sense to you, Jonathan?' he asked.

'Well, er, not really,' said Jonathan candidly.

'Nor to me,' added Roz, smiling as usual, but with an edge to the tone of her voice.

'I'm saying that men must be strong and that women strive to weaken them, tame them, tie them to their aprons. It's a sort of war you know. Yes, a war – a war that some people can conduct with love, but still a war. It's not a man's job to rock the cradle. We must be strong, strong.'

Wally made one more try. 'Veils!' she said dramatically.

The King took up the challenge. 'Well now, consider Fatima,' he said quietly, almost dreamily. 'Fatima, my little pearl, she threw off her veil – I let her do it – and look at all that followed.'

Colonel Moukef, who had listened in silence to the discussion, now raised a hand towards Benahid and a moment later the servants hurried in again and carried the table away. Unexpectedly, the King stood up then and announced that he was retiring for the night. 'Benahid will see to your needs,' he explained. 'Let us meet again in the morning. Good night to you all. Ah, good night Rosemary-Anne.'

The others talked on for a while after the King had gone. Colonel Moukef explained that Benahid and he were loyal to the King, and that there was a palace guard of twenty soldiers who were, well, more or less loyal, though they grumbled a bit. King Abdellah truly was the merest figurehead, stripped of his authority and just useful enough to Youssef Fetouaki and Fatima to be left to rot in his crumbling palace. For his part, Colonel Moukef still hoped the King would fight back some day. 'When he chooses to,' he said with warmth of feeling, 'when the moment comes, I will be there at his side.'

Wally was still looking fussed and seemed to have cut herself out of the conversation. Before long, she rose to her little feet and hurried from the room. Charlie gestured with his thumb towards her. 'Where's the old rock off to then?' he asked casually.

'Yeah,' said Perry, 'a good question. She's looking on the wild side, isn't she? Jonno, keep an eye on her will you. Just see what she's up to.'

'Okay, Perry.' Jonathan hopped up, glad of the excuse to be moving about. Benahid watched, expressionless but alert, as the boy followed Wally out through the door. Jonathan hurried down the inner hall to the foot of the stairs. But Wally wasn't there. So where? He paused to think. Could she have left the palace? One would hardly expect it, after dark and on her own. But when Wally was riled up just about anything was possible. He turned left, walked to the heavy front door, opened it and stepped outside. The courtyard was lit and the two sentries were in their boxes just beyond the door.

'Excuse me,' said Jonathan, looking diffidently from one to the other, 'but have you seen a lady come through here? She's rather, sort of, you'd probably say fat.'

They understood his questions and managed to answer in basic French. 'Oui, oui. La Grande dame. Elle va.' They pointed up the tree-lined approach road.

As he turned to go he heard one of them manage a word or two of English. 'Cigarette? You have cigarette for us?'

'No,' said Jonathan curtly and started to walk briskly along the road. He slowed down suddenly as he realized what he was doing. There were one or two feeble lights set among the trees, but most of the road was very dark. Branches swayed in the evening wind, and when he looked into the shadows between the trees it was like looking into an enormous inkwell. Caves of black. Anything could be lurking there – men, animals, anything. How horrible. The unpleasant chill of fear swept over him. 'Oh blimey,' he said to himself. 'Oh God! It's dark here.' He felt very small. Very alone. Very exposed.

A decision had to be made: To go on, or to turn back? If he went on he would surely soon overtake the puffing Wally. To turn back would probably mean losing her completely. What would Perry and Charlie think about that? They'd know what had really been wrong; that a boy had been scared out of his mind. They wouldn't exactly blame him, in fact Charlie would scrumple his hair or something and say 'Forget it, Jonno' – something like that. But they'd know. Of course they'd know. And then what if poor old Wally, out there on her own, got knocked on her silly head?

He put on more speed. Really, there wasn't a choice; he must go on. His heart started the hideous thump thump thump that goes with fright, and he walked down the centre of the narrow road, forcing himself not to look at the deep shadows on both sides. If something sprang out at him it would just have to go ahead and spring. He tried to reason with himself. There was nothing to be afraid of – just the darkness, and unknown country, and the trees, and the shadows, and hooded Arabs and being along. Catch Wally up. That was the answer. Painfully Jonathan hurried on.

*

Driven by anger, zeal and single-mindedness, Wally was clipping along well. She turned right out of the approach road – ignoring a sentry who seemed to be asleep on the grass – then right again into a narrow road leading down the east side of the palace towards the town centre.

She puffed her way into Avenue Mimoun. The trucks still stood there. A number of men, all wearing traditional Arab rig, were bustling about the place checking loads, canvas cover ties, tyres and other gear. One was working on an engine, revving it up and sending clouds of diesel smoke eddying up the street. There was a strong sense of imminence about the scene. Some sort of conference appeared to be happening round a car parked by an overhead lamp; a big man was leaning against the car, showing a map to the others.

Wally went up to the rearmost lorry. On the driver's door were words that had been crudely scratched out but could still quite easily be read: Bagdesh Transport Company. Three words, and a volume of meaning. Wally's eyes blazed. Bagdesh? That was at least three countries away from Mambay. She moved to the back of the lorry and began tugging at the canvas cover. It wouldn't come away. She found the rope holding it followed it down to the fixing cleat and untied the knot. Jerking the canvas flap aside she peered intently in – and there they were, just discernible in the glimmer of light: the Save Mambay bundles. The supplies she and Sir William had sacrificed so much for in time, effort and money. There lay the life-saving foods, medications and blankets the peasant people out in rural Mambay so badly needed and were never going to see. For once in her embattled life, Wally almost wept.

Then a hand gripped her and held tight. She turned from the truck to see a tall, hooded man there beside her; the white of his eyes and teeth stood out against the darkness of his face and of the night. He seemed angry, and spoke now in guttural Arabic. Wally didn't get a word of it – only the anger came through.

She tried to pull her arm free and failed. 'This is an outrage!' she said, fully matching the tall man's anger with her own. 'It's thievery. I know what's going on and I'll soon put a stop to it. Unload these lorries!'

Jonathan watched as the man hauled her away towards the group assembled under the street-lamp. He was pressed back against the crumbling outer wall of a low building and now, as Wally and the man moved ahead, he slipped forward to the lorry and scrambled underneath it. By kneeling behind the lorry's huge, front right wheel, he could see across towards the group, and even hear much of the Arab chatter going on.

The situation wasn't all that dangerous, he tried to tell himself. Not as dangerous as it looked. They were ordinary men he could see out there in the dim light. If they were dressed differently, like Europeans, if the street weren't quite so dark, if he could understand what was going on – then the fear would go, of course it would. No, but inside himself he knew that wasn't true. These men were bad. The danger was real. He must just control himself as best he could, see it through despite the fear. He leaned forward with his shoulder against the wall of the big tyre, and his cheek touched the knobby rubber of the tread. He still had the blue shorts on and the gritty road was hard on his unprotected knees. He kept very still, watching and listening.

Wally's arrival brought the street-light meeting to a stop. The big man leaning against the car watched in silence as she was dragged across the road and put in front of him. Then the man who'd found her and gripped her arm – which he still held unpleasantly tightly – said something in excited Arabic. There was one word Wally understood: Youssef. So, she'd found him already. The big man standing there, right before her, was the monstrous Youssef Fetouaki himself. He looked the part, built like a mountain and wearing some kind of soldier's uniform. Everything about him had swagger. Wally's pebble eyes levelled some way below his ostentatious show of medal ribbons.

He said something mockingly towards her in Arabic, a leer taking charge of his heavy face.

But Wally had the blaze of anger on her side. 'I don't understand that language,' she said angrily. 'If you want to speak to me, you'll have to do it in English, and this man is hurting my arm. Tell him to let go of me at once.'

Youssef leered on for a moment, then spoke gruffly to the other man, who promptly let go.

'Thank you. Now look here,' Wally went on, 'I know who you are, and what's going on. You're Youssef Fet-something and you're stealing all this stuff' – she waved towards the trucks – 'taking it from the mouths of starving people – starving children. It's cruel, outrageous. How *can* you do it? Well, your racket's over now. Over. Tell your men to unload these lorries. Put the supplies into a safe, dry store until we've worked out a way to deal with distribution. Go on. Do it now.'

The smile faded and open anger, anger mixed with contempt, showed on the dark face. He put his hands on his hips. 'Who the hell are you?' he asked in practised English.

Wally puffed herself up in front of the mountain. '*I*

67

am Mrs Kidwallader Jones,' she said, 'founder of the Save Mambay movement. Those supplies you've been, been *stealing*, came from me, from Sir William Krier and me, and from others too who've sent in money all trying to help, and *you* do this. I'm going straight back to the palace, to the King. You'll hear more about this in the morning, and I'm warning you, don't let those lorries drive away.'

As she turned to go, the other man gripped her arm, that same painful grip, and slowly forced her round to face Youssef again. The leer had come back, and the others in the group began a murmuring laugh, sensing something good about to happen, like spectators at a cockfight as the prize bird flutters into the ring.

Wally kept her nerve. 'How *could* you?' she said accusingly. 'And people *starving*!'

Youssef laughed. 'Let them starve. Let them *all* starve. What do you think they are? I'll tell you, just peasants, ignorant wandering peasants. We don't want 'em – they can die, or go.'

'Tell him to release my arm. I'm going back to the palace at once.'

There was a thoughtful look now. 'You're a very ugly woman,' he said. 'No one could deny that, but I've just been thinking something. My harem's down a bit in numbers. Seven women I think I've got. It's time I had another. And, you know, I think I fancy you. At least you're different. Yes, I think that's what we'll do.' He laughed again, loudly this time, and his huge frame shook. Then he spoke to the rest of the group in laughing Arabic and they all joined in the joke. White teeth showed everywhere against the dark faces as the men rocked about with mirth.

Wally waited until the main bout of cackling was over before taking a whack at Youssef. She stood there alone, but wonderfully defiant, carrying her courage like golden armour. 'You should be ashamed,' she said. 'That is a very poor joke. Dreadful taste. I demand to be released immediately – *immediately*. Now, let me go or I promise you'll regret it.'

She might as well have saved the effort. Youssef laughed again and kept on laughing. Then he patted her on the cheek. 'You'll have a nice time in my harem,' he said. 'It's very comfortable. You'll see – you're going there now.'

Wally did make an effort to struggle when two men began to pull her away into the darkness and to God knows what else – but it didn't amount to much. 'You'll pay a price for this,' she gasped. 'I swear you'll pay. I swear it, swear it.'

Just as they hauled her away, a man in the crowd seemed to have seen the pale face peering out from behind the wheel of a truck. He shouted to Youssef and pointed across the road. Jonathan's thinking mind had nothing to do with his next decision. He sprang out from his cover and ran.

Many voices shouted now. Glancing quickly behind, he saw four or five robed figures chasing after him, and Youssef was pointing and yelling commands. It was hardly an equal contest this, between heavy men in Arab dress and a slight, fit, long-legged boy in shorts – a boy with at least a twenty-yard start. Jonathan surged ahead, increasing his lead each second.

Then two quick bangs, very loud and sharp, shattered the evening air and something crackled past Jonno's bobbing head. Good grief! They were shooting at him now, and one bullet at least had come close.

Like a fleeing antelope, he ran and ran, straining for
speed, hurling himself away from the threatening
hands of Youssef and his men.

Soon his flashing legs took him into the safety of
total darkness and the pursuit seemed to stop. There
were no more shouts; no shots. Just the sound of his
own thumping heart and his soft, plimsolled footsteps,

and his hard breathing to break the silence of the lane. He slowed a bit but kept on running.

The sentries took no notice of the breathless kid who ran across the courtyard and pounded on the palace's front door. Benahid opened it and stood aside as Jonathan stumbled across the threshold into the hall. The others were all standing there looking towards him in surprise.

Charlie hurried forward. 'What the heck's going on, Jonno?' he asked. 'Where've you been?'

Jonathan leaned backwards against the wall and gasped, his cheeks and mouth working away like a suffocating fish. 'It's Wally.' A pause for breath. 'She's out there.' Pause. 'Youssef's got her. He's . . .' Pause. 'He's taking her to his . . .' Pause. 'To his harem.'

'To his *what*?'

Jonathan lowered his head in utter fatigue. 'To his . . .' Pause. 'To his harem,' he repeated.

Now Roz hurried forward. 'Jonno, you look quite done in. Come through to the sitting room here – come and sit down. Get your breath back. Then we'll talk.'

She led him by the hand to one of the low couches and gratefully he flopped on to it. The others gathered round perplexed and silent. A good ten minutes passed before his breathing sounded normal. Even then he was very tired.

'Just tell us what happened,' said Perry softly. 'Then you go off to bed, and we'll try to think of some way out of the mess.'

They listened, aghast, to the story Jonathan had to tell. Then he did go to bed. And exhausted though he was from all that had happened to him that day, he couldn't sleep. His mind was full of the little figure of

Wally standing there before all those bullies. Heroic, that's what she had been. Nothing less. Amazing.

He turned this way and that for an hour or more. In a while gently, gradually, the world began to fade and Jonno fell deeply asleep.

Downstairs, Roz was frantic. Everybody has a breaking point, and she was nearing hers.

Chapter Four

GET WALLY

Nothing was done that night – nothing, that is, except talk, and the talk went on for hours. The Colonel had gone and the King was in bed. Apart from Peregrene, Roz and Charlie, nobody seemed to care a bit about Wally.

They begged Benahid to help – begged him to tell the King what had happened at once. Benahid shook his impassive head, slowly, with great deliberation. 'No,' he said. 'Pas possible.'

'But this is terribly serious,' said Roz frantically raising her voice. 'A dreadful thing. Mrs Kidwallader Jones has been kidnapped – abducted. You *must* help!'

Charlie's moustache was sticking forward again, one way of telling what was going on in his reactive mind. He turned towards Benahid; they were both about the same size and build. 'Where the hell is the Colonel, then?' he demanded. 'Somebody around here is going to have to stir himself.'

Benahid continued to be unmoved. 'The Colonel cannot be reached until morning,' he said. 'Nothing can be done until the morning.'

Charlie put his big red hands on his hips and glowered at the immobile face. He was very aware of the bone-handled dagger sticking out of the sash. A little quiver of his face and hands showed the surge of frustration, of anger flooding through him. Then it seemed to subside. He moved his shoulders in a gesture of helplessness and turned away.

'Benahid, look here.' Perry was drawling away now, being calm – as usual – and polite and to the point. 'We think Mrs Kidwallader Jones is in real danger,' he said. 'She's a very important lady and she's quite an old one. You'll understand that we just want to help, but we're in your hands, absolutely. Is there any way the King can be informed without disturbing him? Could we slide a written note under his door for instance?'

'A note?' Benahid gave the idea his consideration. 'Yes. I will slide a note under his door for you.'

'Great. That's great.' They all murmured with delight at the unexpected good news.

Perry wrote the note in his slow, careful hand. Briefly he described the evening's events, then finished with this request: 'Will you please meet us downstairs to discuss what can be done?'

After Benahid had climbed the King's private stairs with the note, nothing happened for several minutes. Perry, Charlie and Roz sat about the room more or less in silence. Then Benahid returned and handed the note back to Perry. The word 'No' had been written on the bottom. Benahid amplified: 'His Majesty will be pleased to talk to you in the morning,' he said. 'At ten.'

'Jeeze!' murmured Peregrene.

'Really it's outrageous,' said Roz, raising her voice again. 'Unbelievable. Like being back in the dark ages.'

Charlie took the note to see it for himself. 'Good grief!' he snorted. 'Some King. What a feeble man.'

But that was the end for tonight, and at last they went to bed.

Jonathan woke quite early, feeling a little stiff in the thighs, but otherwise fit and refreshed. He thought for a minute or two about Wally again, then pulled on his shorts and shirt and made his way bare-footed to Charlie's room. The servant was out there in the corridor as usual, but took no notice. Quietly, he opened the door and crept in.

Slatted wooden shutters were closed across the window opening. Jonathan swung them open and let the African sunshine stream in. He turned to look at Charlie and was surprised to see him lying there fully clothed but asleep. Charlie grunted now and again, and after two or three minutes opened an eye.

'Hi, Jonno,' he murmured.

'Hi.' Jonathan sat down on the low bed.

'God, what a night.'

'Oh! Have you been drinking or something?'

'Drinking? Hell, no. That's about the only thing they don't seem to do around here. Worse luck.'

'What then?'

'Well, it's just that we couldn't get anything done about the poor old Rock. You'd hardly believe it! The King very kindly said he'd see us about her at ten this morning, and that's all.' Charlie glanced down at the elaborate navigator's watch on his wrist. 'It's still only seven-fifteen. *Seven-fifteen!* What the heck have you got me up so early for, anyway?'

Jonathan grinned. 'Er, you see, I woke up, and I—'

'Yeah. I know. You wanted a little company. Okay mate.' He swung his legs off the bed and stood up.

Downstairs they met Benahid again and Charlie

nudged the boy. 'D'you think he ever sleeps?' he whispered.

'I dunno.'

'Morning, Benahid,' said Charlie amiably. 'Can you let us out to have a stroll in the palace grounds?'

Benahid bowed slightly. 'Please follow me,' he said, and led the way through a huge room furnished for conferences, then on through a door in the east side of the palace, and into the open air.

It was truly beautiful out there. Droplets of dew glittered on the grass blades, the sun, huge-looking and blazing as Jonno had never seen it blaze before, hung in an utterly clear sky; he felt the piercing strength of the rays on his face and legs despite a morning coolness still in the air. 'Blimey, Charlie,' he said, 'what a day.'

'Yeah. It's going to be a cooker. Don't get burnt, mate.'

Relaxed now, and happy in each other's company, they strolled through the palace gardens. Beyond a group of trees, they found a run-down little zoo with a handful of mangy animals gazing sadly out at them. Wandering back, they came across a partly dried-out lake and then, just behind the palace, what seemed to be a secret ornamental garden which they peeped at through a tiny, gilded gate.

Jonathan saw it first. 'Look, Charlie,' he said. 'That seems funny. What's it doing here, all shut away?'

'Yeah, well, I think I know. I bet it was for the King's womenfolk, when the poor old boy had some. Have a sniff. It's like Woolworth's perfumery.'

Jonathan sniffed and turned away. 'Crumbs, it's getting hot,' he said.

'Hot is right – let's go back in. I want some break-fast.'

'What d'you think they'll give us?'

'I don't know. Something tasty, I'm sure. How does boiled goat grab you?'

'Blimey, I hope not.'

In the hall they met Roz and Perry, then all went through to eat together. Breakfast turned out to be croissants, jam and coffee. Not the sort of breakfast Jonno was used to but not bad either, not at all bad, and very much better than goat.

At about a quarter to ten, Colonel Moukef arrived and shook hands politely. Roz began to babble on about Wally, but the Colonel raised a hand, and she paused. 'I know about Mrs Kidwallader Jones,' he said.

They were all surprised to hear it. 'You *know*?' queried Roz. 'Well, then, is anything being done?'

'It's very hard to see what can be done. Youssef is – is a power in Mambay.'

Perry spoke next. 'Is there a foreign legation here?' he asked. 'An American consul perhaps, or British, or French – is any western power represented here?'

Moukef shook his head. 'No. Youssef sent most of the diplomats home long ago. The ones still here are his friends.'

'Well, I don't know what we should do – goddammit I just don't know.'

At five to ten, Benahid led them to the conference room where King Abdellah joined them at exactly ten o'clock. The King sat on one side of the long table with Colonel Moukef beside him. Perry, Charlie and Roz faced him, tensely.

'I hope you all enjoyed a good night's sleep,' said the King politely.

Roz, pale and unsmiling, caught his eye. 'Your Majesty,' she said, 'I hardly slept at all. I am most concerned about Mrs Kidwallader Jones.'

'Yes, you look tired my dear. I'm so sorry. Perhaps there is something you can take. You know, Rosemary-Anne, I have been thinking very much about you. I have a son, Yacoub, a fine young man, a soldier and horseman. He is twenty-three and has only two wives, which is not a great number for a man like Yacoub. Yacoub is a man of moderation, and you will like him very much. You see, it has come into my mind that you, Rosemary-Anne, would make an excellent wife for my son. Now, how does that sound – wife of a crowned prince – good, eh? You are tempted?'

Roz controlled herself at the cost of enormous inner effort. 'You honour me greatly,' she said. 'I am deeply grateful. But, Your Majesty, about Mrs Kidwallader Jones—'

'I will send for Yacoub. He is a good son. He will come when his father calls. You will meet and talk together and decisions will be made. Welcome to my family, Rosemary-Anne.' He smiled indulgently across the table, and Roz, defeated for the moment, blushed despite her weariness.

Then Charlie hit the table a hard blow with the side of his heavy fist, and everyone looked towards him. The King's smile lingered unchanged for a second or so, then slowly faded as the royal eyes swung from Roz and her delicate blush to the looming anger of Charlie's face.

'Now listen, King Abdellah,' said Charlie bluntly. 'We've had about enough of this cods. We want Mrs Kidwallader Jones back in one piece, that is, if she isn't dead already. So what are you going to do?'

A suffocating silence followed, and Jonathan felt a tremor flicker up his spine. He didn't like the King's sudden glassiness, or the way Moukef was staring across the table, sharp and watchful, like a panther stalking its prey. It was all so weird, like playing with a bomb; you could go from nothing happening to calamity in one rash move – what a mess, what an awkward, dangerous mess. Charlie's moustache was also signalling clearly that he wasn't finished yet.

'I'm putting it to you straight,' Charlie went blundering on, not reading the warning signs at all. 'We want her out today, or we'll have the whole flippin' United Nations army out here to get her back. Come on King Abdellah – just what are you actually going to do? And do *now*?'

Moukef rose slowly to his feet, still staring at Charlie. He was on the King's left side. On Abdellah's other flank, Benahid appeared from somewhere and seemed to arrive in an effortless sideways glide. One way and the other it was looking quite bad. The tremors flickered on in Jonathan's bones uncomfortably.

Then Perry went through his cooling patter again. 'Mr Thompson doesn't mean to upset you, sir,' he explained, 'but can something please be done immediately – today, this morning?'

The King warmed a little. 'Perhaps,' he said. 'I think so. Soon at least. I think we can get your lady friend out.'

'How?' Roz asked the question passionately.

'Well, you see, Youssef has enemies, many enemies. He knows some day they will strike and so, though he is by no means a coward, he is always ready to run. He has many means of escape. In his harem, for instance, right in the main hall where his women gather to while away the boredom of their days, there is an entrance to a tunnel. No one knows of it. The entrance is hidden beneath a marble statue. It is always locked, but

I have a key — Fatima's key. Fatima thinks she lost the key, and she never dared to tell Youssef.' He gave another of his dry little chuckling laughs. 'Poor Fatima. She is still so afraid of Youssef.'

'Sir,' said Perry. 'You are saying we can get Mrs Kidwallader Jones away through that escape route. Can you go on? How do we do it? To start with, how do we reach her?'

The King looked across at Moukef, who had gone back to his seat. 'You are a soldier, Colonel,' he said. 'What is your plan of campaign?'

'Your Majesty, it should not be difficult. People wishing rewards from Youssef do sometimes take a girl of beauty to join his harem. If the lady here, Rosemary-Anne, would consent to, ah, to pretend to join the harem, I think she should be able to lead Mrs Kidwallader Jones to safety.'

Charlie shook his head. 'No,' he said flatly. 'We've lost one already and we're not losing Roz.'

Then Roz had her say. 'Yes, I'll do it. If we can choose a moment when we know Youssef is away I won't be in danger from him — not until he gets back. By then we'll be out and away.'

'No,' said Perry. 'I agree with Charlie. It's too big a risk, Roz.'

'Nonsense! I'm going to do it. There's no other way. We've got to get Wally out. Yes, Colonel, I'll do it.'

'No.' Now it was the King. He gave a little negative wave of his head, and said the word again with firmness. 'No.'

'But, Your Majesty—'

'*No*. For Yacoub's sake I cannot allow it. The matter is at an end. Moukef, what other suggestion do you have?'

Moukef paused to consider the effect of the King's veto. 'It is now more difficult, Your Majesty,' he said quietly. 'However, I think the principle of smuggling a young lady into the harem should be maintained. It seems to me to be that or a full attack, which would take some preparation. Perhaps there is another girl we could persuade . . .'

'Hmm.' The King was looking thoughtful, too. 'This girl. She needs three qualities – does she not? – youth, beauty and dependability. They seldom come to-gether.'

'That is so, sir. You see, there is my niece—'

'Moukef, your relations – those I have seen – are all distinguished by their ugliness. By some odd chance you, yourself, have pleasant features – but the others – and in particular, your women! No, Moukef, I can-not think a niece of yours will do.'

'I agree, sir. You say no more than the truth.'

'So?'

'So, I must think, must have a little time to think.'

The King smiled unexpectedly. 'You don't see the answer then?'

'Er, no, sir. At present, I do not.'

'Well, I do, and the answer is staring directly at you, now – there.' He pointed a bony finger towards Jona-than. '*There* is your answer.'

'The boy?'

'Of course. Look at him.'

'Yes, yes. I see. Dress him as a girl. Of course, Your Majesty, he has a pleasant beardless face, long hair, good eyes. I think it ought to work, an excellent idea.'

Jonathan's cheeks turned scarlet as the full signifi-cance of what the King had said – and said so casually – sank home, and there the wretched man seemed con-

81

tent to leave it. His Royal flipping Highness had sorted everything out in a sentence or two and was rising from the table.

'Time to go back to my books,' King Abdellah murmured. 'Work your plans out, all of you; let me know about them later. Moukef, write me a report about it all. And I will be pleased to see everyone for dinner tonight, at six-thirty.' The royal audience was at an end.

Moukef got quickly to his feet as the King started to go and then, one by one, so did the others, feeling awkward and uncertain. Halfway across the room, the King stopped, turned, smiled directly, meaningfully towards Roz, then walked on.

Events had moved so fast they had rather left Charlie behind. Now, as the door closed behind the King, anger came welling out of him like an oil strike. 'What kind of loony nonsense is this?' he demanded, the hairs of his moustache quivering and sticking forward like a little red cornfield. 'Did I hear right? *Did I?* Did the King say Jonathan was going into that ruddy harem of Youssef's? Over my dead body, he is, Moukef, over my dead body!'

Moukef began to look dangerous. It was obvious he didn't care for public displays of anger, and especially not when disrespectful talk about the King came into them. Still standing, he glowered into Charlie's eyes. 'Dead bodies are not too difficult to arrange here,' he said. 'We used to stick the heads on posts in the market square.'

Then, predictably, Perry came in with his balm-oil and reasonableness – the usual routine. 'Charlie, Charlie,' he said softly. 'Cut it out, man. Shouting off your mouth like that doesn't help anything, now does it? We've got a real awkward situation here – god-dammit, let's all just sit down and talk sensibly. Let's *get* somewhere.'

They spent at least an hour going over the possibilities. Really, there weren't many, but during the talk Jonathan's emotions were exposed and wracked and stretched and abused until he'd just about gone through the whole gamut of feelings a $13\frac{1}{2}$-year-old can manage. There had been humiliation, fear, a sort of duty-glow, moments of heroic fancy and overlaying it all a sense of helplessness; that whatever must be, must be.

Charlie fought on for a while against Moukef's plan. His plan was a break-in by Perry and himself. Not much subtlety to it, of course, as you'd expect from Charlie. He came back to the theme three times at least, but with less and less conviction. Each time Moukef explained why it couldn't be done, and that both men would probably die in the attempt. Youssef's harem was about as pregnable as Fort Knox. The others listened mostly in silence, putting a word in here and there and searching their minds vainly for a new and better way to spring Wally.

Moukef had no doubts – positively none. Jonathan could easily be made to look like a girl, and easily slipped into the harem. An hour or two later he would be safely out again, with Mrs Kidwallader Jones behind him. There was no real risk this way. Nothing more to the whole thing than a clear brief and good timing, matters that would be fully taken care of. The boy would be told exactly what to do and when to do it. Finally, as he and the lady came out of the escape tunnel, they would find a car waiting; in it would be Mr Langhorne and Mr Thompson. The four of them would drive at speed to Yankee Foxtrot. Miss Hart would already have been taken there by himself, Moukef, and would be seated in the aircraft. They would start the engines and go. Presto! Like that. Problem solved. The sheer soldier's confidence of the man had its effect.

In the end they all agreed. Perhaps it would be truer to say of Charlie that he stopped disagreeing. When he saw the drift of the situation he simply got up from the table, walked to the window and stood there, in silence, his big red hands expressively on his hips. Then Perry put the question that had to come.

'Well, Jonno, what d'you say? D'you think you can do it?'

Jonathan reddened again, looked down at the table and said 'Yes, Perry. I'll do it. I mean, really, I have to – haven't I?' The words came out as a whisper. Charlie looked round, then looked back again towards the window. He said nothing.

Moukef smiled. 'Good,' he said. 'The King will be pleased with you. Now, let's get on with it as fast as we can. I'll find out where Youssef is this evening. If he's away on what he calls "business" – which I think he is – we can get going at once. I'll look out some clothes for the boy. Then there's the question of who takes him along, gives him away so to speak. Rather an important point that. Yes, I know, just the man: Sergeant Houmman. I'll speak to him. Now, let me see, let me see – I suggest we meet here again at three o'clock. Is that agreed?'

They all nodded, except for Charlie, who seemed to have cut himself out of the conversation and was still at the window. After Moukef left it was all a bit awkward for a moment or two; a bit strained.

84

Roz walked up to Charlie. 'I know how you feel,' she said softly. 'We don't want Jonno in there either. I'd give an eyebrow to be doing it myself – honestly, but the way things are, we don't seem to have a choice, and I do think it'll work out all right. Don't worry too much.'

When Charlie turned round he had a grin on his face, a big, genuine, teeth-showing affair. 'Look,' he said, 'just dress me up as a bit of Mambay crumpet, and *I'll* do it. I'm better looking than Jonno anyway – that's obvious.'

Everybody smiled then, and Jonathan laughed out loud. 'Blimey,' he said, 'I reckon you'd be enough to make even Youssef run.'

They idled the hours away pleasantly enough, apart from a tenseness that came and went in waves and affected them all. A bit of chat went on, but not about the ordeal lying ahead; not a word was said about that.

Roz snuggled up to Perry in the sun, resting her head on his stomach and he ran his lean fingers through her hair. Some weird noises came from one of the mangy animals in the zoo; a monkey suffering from the heat perhaps.

Just before three, Benahid came out to say that Colonel Moukef had arrived. They stood up, and Jonathan went very pale. He looked away from the others, but Charlie had noticed and putting a hand on his hair, tilted the boy's head back and looked into his eyes.

'We'll be waiting for you, Jonno,' he said, 'just outside, a stone's throw away, and if there's any trouble, we'll come busting in like a couple of Sherman tanks – that's a promise.'

Moukef greeted them politely in the King's sitting room. 'Youssef is away and not expected back until late tomorrow,' he said. 'I suggest we go straight on with the plan.'

Perry seemed doubtful. 'You're sure about Youssef?' he asked.

'Pretty sure. Sergeant Houmman is waiting in the hall. And I have some clothes here – look.' He pointed to a mainly black bundle of silk-like material. 'It's good-quality stuff,' he explained. 'From my sister – for her daughters. It should fit.' He separated the bundle out into its different parts. There were trousers that narrowed towards the ankles, a long smock of a dress and a cowl that fitted over the wearer's head and spread across the shoulders. There was a green object, too, trimmed with lace. 'The veil,' explained Moukef. 'It buttons across the front of his face, just above the nose.'

Jonathan studied it all in silent misery.

'There won't be much of him to see,' went on the Colonel, 'but, of course, once he's in the harem, they'll take the veil off. Well, let's get on with it, Jonathan. Put the clothes on. You'd better go up to your room.'

Jonathan hesitated, swallowed twice, glanced towards Charlie, then gathered the stuff up into his arms and walked off towards the stairs. In about ten minutes the door opened slowly and he came back. Or someone with Jonathan's face – although even that seemed to have changed. He'd put everything on except the veil, which he held in his hand. There he stood, looking at them one by one, and an electrifying silence fell. Even Moukef was affected for the moment. In place of an exuberant schoolboy stood a grave, white-faced North African girl with centuries of sadness and hardship

86

gazing out of darkly vivid eyes. The transformation
was extraordinary; and oddly moving.

Moukef rallied first. 'That's fine,' he said. 'Everything seems to fit very well. I thought it would. Now,
let's try putting on the veil.'

The green bit of cloth with its lace trimmings buttoned easily into place, leaving only a narrow band of Jonathan's face to be seen. The eyes seemed bigger than ever now, and sadder and more compelling against the shiny green and blackness of the clothing and the whiteness of the skin around them.

'Yes, that's very good,' Moukef went on, unbuttoning the veil. 'No one would ever guess. Now, let's just sit down for a moment all together and run over exactly what it is we're about to do.'

At about a quarter past four Jonathan, renamed Leila, left with Sergeant Houmman for the harem. He went abruptly and without ceremony – nothing more than a mumbled 'Good-bye', vaguely addressed to everyone. His eyes were very bright as he turned to go, and it was obvious, even with the veil buttoned tightly into place, that he was on the point of tears. He left an oppressive atmosphere of gloom behind him.

The journey to Youssef's fortress-like house was done on foot – about three miles in the hot sun. They walked in silence and at speed. Houmman, not dressed as a soldier, seemed to want to get the job over with, and clipped along faster than Jonathan could comfortably manage. The veil was a nuisance. It stuck to the boy's cheeks, soaked by sweat from his forehead which squeezed out from under the cowl and rolled down to reach the veil. The wretched thing even clogged his mouth and nose, and made breathing difficult.

Youssef's vast, Moorish house was set behind railings, and in beautiful grounds. Behind the railings, themselves very tall and strong, was an ugly wall of coiled barbed wire and a deep ditch. At an opening in the railings, a checkpoint had been set up, guarded by two foot soldiers and two cannon-firing army scout cars.

Houmman chattered away in rapid Arabic to the sentries, who grinned at Jonathan coarsely, then waved them through. Another soldier slid up from somewhere and escorted them on through the inner gardens to Youssef's most private of private quarters. The soldier thumped on a heavy, wooden door and stood aside. They waited.

After a while, the door opened and an immensely fat man stepped out to meet them. Houmman began his Arabic routine again, talking, it seemed, from somewhere below his Adam's apple, and the fat man listened, asking questions from time to time and nodding thoughtfully. At last he reached towards Jonathan, unbuttoned the veil with pudgy hands and peeled the soaking cloth aside. For a second or two, his deeply sunk eyes studied Jonathan's face, then he released the veil which swung down out of the way; it was good just to feel the cooling air down as low as your chin. The man was talking to Houmman again. Evidently he approved because they laughed together several times.

Jonathan knew what the story was to be. Houmman had found this young girl; she was from far away – it wasn't possible to say where, perhaps French Africa somewhere. Anyway, she didn't speak Arabic. Houmman would be glad to part with her – er, for a favour or two from Youssef. He would call back in a week. Perhaps there would be some news for him then – good news that would make life for a poor man a little easier.

With startling abruptness, Houmman turned and left. There was no word of farewell, not even a nod. Just his rear view disappearing at the same fast clip, back towards a safer part of the town. The hollow feeling came to Jonathan's gut again. He desperately wanted to run, to chase after Houmman, and beg him not to be left in this place.

Then his arm was taken firmly by the fat man who pulled him inside to the coolness of the harem. The great door shut and at first it seemed rather dark which was quite a relief. His eyes adjusted quickly and he saw he was in a great, tiled entrance hall. The man went on pulling, and they passed through a doorway into something that was almost too much to believe.

They were in a spacious, colourful hall strewn with rugs and couches and exotic plants – all so lavish it made you wonder if your mind was giving up the struggle and leading you to a private cuckoo-land of your own invention. A fountain was playing at one end of the room – to his right – and he caught a glimpse of fish swimming in a pond of crystal clarity. At the finish of a hot, blistering day it was wonderfully cool in here; so cool he felt a shiver run unexpectedly through him.

At the other end of the room, a small group of women were sitting, taking mint tea with each other and chatting. One was doing more chatting than the others – a lot more. She was a little fat figure, rather wild looking and incongruous in her harem-clothes.

Mostly she was speaking English with a few words of dreadful French thrown in. 'You are what you eat,' she said. 'I keep on telling you. And if you ate better food you'd be doing something to change all this. I'm not finished with Youssef, you know! I'm most certainly not.'

'Oh blimey!' murmured Jonathan to himself as the words came cutting through the gentle air and sound of splashing water to reach him. 'It's her. And she's still at it.'

He hardly noticed at the time, but Wally's fighting words took most of the unpleasant feeling out of his gut. For one thing, he wasn't alone.

Chapter Five

PURSUIT

The fat man pulled Jonathan on through the great room, between two rows of brightly painted pillars supporting the roof. As they went, he called out towards the group of women and one of them left the tea party and came towards them. She was darkly good-looking and very young. Sixteen, Jonathan decided, at the most seventeen. She had violet eyes, sharply formed features and long black hair that reached down to the small of her back. The fat man and the girl spoke to each other in French, and Jonathan understood just enough to see a new problem coming.

Soon the fat man walked away and he was left with the girl. She smiled and patted him reassuringly on the shoulder. 'Parle-tu français?' she asked.

'Er, no. Non. Not much anyway. English.'

'Ah well, I can manage a little of that,' she said. 'We will talk in English. Good practice for me.' She had a very pleasant way of speaking – accented and musical. 'My name is Tasma,' she went on.

'Oh yes. I see. How do you do – and mine's—'

'I know, Leila.'

'Eh? Yes, of course. That's right.' Good grief, but that had been a near one, thought Jonathan. With so much going on he'd forgotten his new name. Another second and he'd have burbled out the real one – and then what?

'Anyway, Leila, I'm to help you have a bath. You look as if you would like one.'

Now he was being pulled along again. By Tasma this time. They were moving towards a door at the back of the main room while Jonathan groped frantically about in his mind for a way out of this bit of awkwardness.

'Really, thank you, I don't think I want a bath,' he said.

'But of course you do. Look at you! You have been very hot. You will feel much, much better after a bath.'

They were actually in the bathroom now — and what a place it was, fully three times the size of Jonathan's bathroom at home, and with turquoise tiles on the floor and marvellously ornate decorations. The bath itself was gilded, and sunk to about half its depth below floor level.

'No, no. Really. I ...' Jonathan was scarlet in the face now and out of control again.

Tasma was looking at him in surprise, aware of his deep embarrassment. 'You mean,' she began. 'Is it that you don't want my help?'

'Well, yes. Thank you very much but I'd — I'd rather — if you don't mind I'd—'

She laughed lightly. 'You're just shy. You are silly. I'll get you a towel then, and leave you, if that's what you want.'

Jonathan's embarrassment was slow to subside. He felt such an ass. Dreadful the humiliations he got into. When Tasma came back with the towel, he found it hard to look her in the face. 'Thanks,' he mumbled, and held it without moving.

'D'you want a change of clothes?'

'Er, no. No thank you. These will do. And – thanks.'

'That's all right,' she said, her vivid eyes searching his out determinedly and lingering on then for a moment. 'I think I understand. Don't drown.' She walked away smiling, and closed the door, leaving him alone.

He slipped luxuriously into the hot water, lay back and closed his eyes. 'You will feel much, much better', Tasma had said – and she was right. Gentle waves of pleasure swept over him. Odd how much a hot bath did for you – so much more than cleaning the body; it worked on the mind too, made you feel safe and serene. Yes, but he mustn't linger long. Someone might come at any moment.

Soon he sat up, soaped himself, washed the soap off with a huge, fluffy sponge, got dried and dressed.

As he reached for the door handle, he saw something that surprised him. The door was very slightly open. Anxiety returned.

Cautiously, he put his head out and looked right and left into the little lobby beyond the bathroom door. Relief, there was nobody there. He stepped out, through the lobby and on into the great, pillared room. He turned left, steering away from the wives towards some reclining chairs grouped beside the pond and statue – the statue he was going to have to move to get Wally out.

The chairs had little wheels at the front and handles at the back, to make them easy to move about. They looked most inviting and restful. You could stretch out full length in them – which seemed a good idea. Jonathan rolled comfortably on to one while he thought out the next move. He could hear Wally's voice still; a bit muffled from here, but still raving on. She seemed to be trying to start some sort of palace revolution. Well, she would of course. Anyway, she didn't seem to be getting far. The other wives obviously found this quaint, English-speaking newcomer amusing to listen to, but not much more than that. Out of the corner of his eye he could assess the attention they were paying; you would call it anything but rapt.

Then, suddenly, there was a movement beside him, and another reclining chair appeared very close. Tasma, smiling knowingly, lay down on it. She put a hand across, took hold of Jonathan's and gave it several little squeezes.

'Hello,' she said.

Jonathan couldn't think where to look, and felt his cheeks turn red again; for once he'd have liked to hide behind the suffocating veil.

'Er, hello,' he managed to reply.

'So what have you come here for?' There was something distinctly funny about the way she looked at him. And the squeezing went on.

'What? Oh well. I mean, like – like you, er, I've—'

'Don't be silly! You're not like me.' She giggled very quietly. 'You're a boy. Don't try it on any more. You see, I peeped.'

'You – you mean, while I was—'

'Of course.' Another little giggle.

So that's why the bathroom door had been slightly open. His face felt like a two-kilowatt electric fire by now, and he turned his head away towards the wall – the meanness of it. She'd crept back when he thought he was alone, and spied on him – the humiliation of it. Damn her and her little treachery! And what now? In God's name what was going to happen now?

'Go on. Tell me then. What's it all about?'

'No. I – look, go away. Please. Leave me alone.'

There was more giggling. Very quiet. Almost a whisper. When she spoke next, she seemed to be taunting him.

'Know what they'll do to you if they catch you?'

Jonathan decided not to answer and just kept staring at the wall.

'You see, men aren't allowed in here; not real men – except Youssef, and the same goes for boys. Look – look over there.'

Painfully, Jonathan turned his head and looked.

'Those fat men over there aren't real men, you know. They're eunuchs.' She giggled again, enjoying the whole thing. 'Got some missing parts. And that's what they'll do to you if they catch you. I mean, if I tell them.'

Jonathan moved his eyes in misery to meet hers. 'You *wouldn't*,' he whispered.

'I might. In fact, I *will* unless you tell me what you're here for.'

Jonathan swallowed two or three times, hardly aware of the hand-squeezing still going on. It was game, set and match to Tasma, and he knew it, and she knew it, and he knew she knew it.

'All right,' he said. 'I'll tell you, if you promise to keep it a secret.'

'I promise,' she giggled. 'I won't tell.'

'Well, I'm here to rescue that fat lady over there. The one doing all the talking. Wally we call her. There's a secret way out of here, and I've got the key to it. I've to get her through a tunnel to a car. Then we drive to the airport where we've got an Aztec waiting.'

'A what?'

'You know, an aeroplane. Twin engines. We flew in it the other day. I'm with two pilots – they're great. They really can fly. You should see them. I can fly too, of course, but I'm not old enough to have a licence.'

The embarrassment was fading fast. Pleasant to be able to talk freely to someone. Even to Tasma.

'You're Jonathan, aren't you? Jonathan Pane or something.'

'Jonathan Kane. How did you know?'

'I heard your friend Wally mention you – you and the others. I thought it might be you, almost from the start.'

'Well, keep quiet about it. I want to get going soon.'

'All right. I'm coming too.'

Jonathan was aghast. 'You – you're what? But you can't! You know you can't.'

She started to get up off the couch. 'I'm going to tell one of those eunuchs who you are,' she said blandly. 'They'll tear you to pieces.'

'No. Wait.' Jonathan grabbed her hand and pulled her back beside him. 'Please! I'd take you with me if I could, honestly, but I just can't, now can I?'

'Why not? Of course you can. What's more, you're going to, or I'll tell the eunuchs.'

'Blimey! Oh hell! You really are – I mean I don't know what a ruddy well . . . Blimey. All right, I suppose you'll have to come too. But, listen, if you mess it up, I'll—'

'You'll what?' Another giggle. 'If we mess it up, the eunuchs will be on you like a pack of dogs. They won't do anything to me.'

She stopped squeezing his hand and began to stroke it. 'You be nice to Tasma,' she said coquettishly.

'For Pete's sake, all right! Gosh – one of those eunuchs is looking over here.'

'Don't worry about him. That old fella can't see more than about the length of his arm. Anyway, what's the plan?'

'The plan. Yes, well, first we've got to slide that statue aside. The entrance to the tunnel should be underneath it. Then I've got to find a way to talk to Wally, you know, to explain. Then, when nobody's looking we slip out through the tunnel.'

It sounded a bit lame, as Jonathan himself realized.

'You're even sillier than I thought,' said Tasma. 'When nobody's *looking*! Dear mother of a saint! When do you think that's going to be? Have you seen how many eunuchs are in here on guard?'

'Er, yes. We thought there wouldn't be so many. We thought two or so.'

'There are six. Six! And you think you can push the heavy statue aside and get old Wally what-ever-her-name-is down the hole with nobody noticing. I'll tell you something, clever boy. You need me. You *really* need me.'

'Colonel Moukef seemed to feel it would be easy.'

'Pfaf! Now, I'll tell you what we're going to do. I'll get Wally to come over to see you. Then I'll spill a potful of mint tea on the floor and tell a eunuch that I want to clean it up. While we're doing that, we'll move the statue and unlock the door – we can make a sort of barricade of chairs to screen us.

'Now comes the hard bit. I'll go over to that end of the room and cause a scene – I'll get everyone fighting and yelling. While the eunuchs are busy sorting that out, you and the old woman go down the hole, and go quickly. I'll follow. Is that agreed?'

'Agreed,' said Jonathan gratefully. 'Thanks.'

'Good. Now, let's get on with it.'

She rolled off the long chair and strolled casually towards Wally, over in the main sitting area. Two or three minutes later she came strolling back. She had Wally and a pot of tea with her.

'So it is you,' Wally said. 'How on earth did you get in here?'

Jonathan smiled uncertainly. 'They dressed me up as a girl. I'm supposed to be another of Youssef's wives or something.'

'Huh! It wouldn't be difficult. Perhaps that'll teach you to get your hair cut. Where are the others then?' The little pebble eyes were giving him the old one-two again, nothing had changed.

'They're outside in a car. At least, Perry and Charlie are. Are you all right?'

'Of course I'm all right, perfectly all right. Terrible food they live on in here, but the bread is quite healthy. Whole wheat germ. That's all I've eaten. Where's Roz?'

'She's supposed to be at the airport, waiting. You see, I know a way to escape from here, and all we've got to do is get to the car, then run for it. We're, well, you know, saving you from Youssef.' It seemed important to bring the point out.

'Youssef? Bosh! It takes more than Youssef to frighten me. He hasn't even had the nerve to come and see me yet. What about that? *And* he's got some shocks coming to him when he does appear. I'll have all his wives against him by then. I'll soon show *him* what he is! A nothing.'

'Blimey!' said Jonathan. 'You're going on as much as ever, aren't you?' Even her head was jerking about again.

'And I see you're as rude as ever,' she snapped.

'You'd better stop it. Don't be a rude little boy.'

Tasma raised a cautionary finger, then let go of the pot, and it clattered on to the hard floor, letting a large amount of mint tea flow round the base of the statue. 'Look what I've done,' she moaned. 'How clumsy of me. Move the chairs, and I'll get a mop to clean up with.'

She hurried over to the eunuchs' quarters near the main entrance, and came back with a long-handled mop and a pail of water. Wally and Jonathan had stacked three of the reclining chairs on top of each other and placed them to break the line of sight from the far end of the room.

'Let's hurry,' said Tasma. 'One of these nosey eunuchs will be over before long. Come on, help me push the statue clear.' With an effort, they slid the heavy bronze figure to the side and there, just as it should be, was the trap door. 'Unlock it,' whispered Tasma.

Jonathan groped for the key in a little pocket beneath his dress, and dropped to his hands and knees. The door unlocked easily and swung open to show a vertical ladder set into the old stone foundation walling. Through the half-dark he could see a tunnel leading away westwards, passing underneath the bathrooms block. He turned his head slowly to look at Wally, who was stooped, peering at the top of the ladder, her hands on her knees.

'Crikey!' he murmured.

'Ssh . . .' warned Tasma. 'You go first, Leila – I mean, Jonathan. Guide her feet on to the rungs with your hands. But wait till I've started my bit of confusion – Oh, Sacré Coeur! One of the eunuchs is coming. Be busy.'

She swung away and walked smilingly towards the fat man rolling towards them. The two met on collision courses and bumped together. Tasma said something jokingly, tickled him under his several chins with her forefinger, then linked her arm through his and playfully steered him away, back towards the other end of the room. Jonathan, in full alarm, watched from the side of his eyes. 'Blimey,' he whispered, his heart thumping. 'Did you see that?'

Wally was down on her knees making a feeble show of cleaning the floor and puffing already. 'No, I didn't,' she said. 'And if you use that dreadful word "blimey" once more, I'll smack you. And I don't care who's watching.'

A sudden shriek rang out from the end of the room. Jonathan glanced round the piled chairs for a quick look at the action. One of the wives had the bucket upside down on her head and was standing, dripping, in a pool of water. Then, from behind a pillar, the wet end of the mop swung suddenly out to hit another wife's behind, sending her stumbling into contact with a startled-looking eunuch. Tasma began screaming at the other women, accusing them of provoking trouble, and soon there was wholesale hair-pulling, face slapping, swearing and hysteria where the solemn tea party had been happening a few minutes before.

Jonathan gazed in amazement, then jerked himself back to reality. 'Come on,' he urged. 'Quick. Follow me.'

Nimbly, he slid through the trap door opening, and started down the ladder. Wally approached the ordeal on her hands and knees slowly, like a large ship entering harbour. She turned and advanced rear end first towards the top rung. Looking up, Jonathan saw her little feet appear, suspended in space above him. 'Hurry!' he hissed. 'For God's sake.'

Hesitantly, gropingly, she lowered her right leg until Jonathan grabbed her ankle and pulled it down, putting her toes in contact with the third rung. 'Now, the next one – come on.' It swung about for a moment, then came down, and he grabbed that ankle, too, and pushed her foot to the fourth rung. Wally's belly still supporting most of her weight, was pressed against the floor on the hard edge of the opening.

'Put your hands on the ladder,' he whispered, 'and hold on. For Pete's sake, make an effort.' Wally gripped the top rung so tightly that her knuckles went white. She was making just about the biggest effort of her life.

As they reached the foot of the ladder, they heard feet running above them and then, with startling suddenness, Tasma sprang through the opening. Cat-like, she raced down the rungs, paused mid-way to slam the trap door shut, then raced on.

'I loused that up,' she said. 'They're after us. Go on, run!'

The exit tunnel had a musty smell and was very dark. Jonathan started down it, heading towards a dim square of light at the far end. Annoyingly the roof was lower than head height, and they had to run in an awkward, stooped position. Wally kept up the gasping and gave whispered cries of distress. 'Oh my!' she moaned. Gasp. 'Oh, dear me.' Gasp. 'Oh dear.'

'Come *on*,' yelled Jonathan. He was leading, running half-turned towards her, tugging her along by her left wrist. Tasma nudged gently from behind and whispered encouragement. 'Keep going,' she urged. 'That's just fine. You're doing well.' Wally's little feet twinkled along faster than they had gone in more than fifty years. Noises from the rear showed that the eunuchs had opened the trap door and were coming down in pursuit. Fortunately, their shape was hardly better than Wally's for getting down the ladder.

The square of light turned out to be a louvred panel in an old wooden door. Jonathan took hold of an iron handle, turned it, and pushed with his shoulder. The door moved. He pushed harder. It opened fully, scraping away a layer of stony ground as it went. Jonathan felt a surge of joy run through him. They were in the open – in the sweet fresh air again. The first signs of darkness were in the sky.

'Go on,' hissed Tasma from behind.

Automatically, Jonathan reached for Wally's wrist, and hauled her through the door. They were in an area of scrubland now, with a path leading through it. The painful running began again then, suddenly, Wally shook her wrist free. 'Let go of me,' she gasped. 'I'm not running any more.' Puff, gasp.

'But the eunuchs. They're coming after us,' protested Jonathan.

'I don't care.' Puff. 'Let them come.'

'Listen – what's that, Tasma?' Whistles were sounding in the distance.

'That's the alarm. They're calling out the soldiers. Come on, Wally, try again. Just one more big effort.'

Wally did her best. They lurched on through cactus growths and stunted fig trees and then, suddenly, there it was; a five-year-old Citroen, painted grey and layered with reddish dust. Charlie was standing idly near the front, leaning backwards against the right-hand wing. Perry was inside, at the wheel, looking comfortable and relaxed.

Jonathan let out a great, excited whoop. 'Char-lee, it's us!'

Charlie sprang away from the car and ran a few paces towards them. 'Great stuff, Jonno,' he said. 'You've got her, then – got the old rock? My God, she looks rough.'

The old rock was hissing air in and out so fast she couldn't speak a word. Perry opened the back door and she collapsed into the car.

Charlie's eyes focused on Tasma. 'And who the hell are you?' he asked.

'I'm Tasma. I'm going with you. But don't bother about me now. Let's get moving. They'll be after us at any moment.'

Jonathan looked awkwardly away. 'I had to bring her,' he explained. 'She made me.'

Charlie turned to Jonno and Tasma. 'Get in, you two,' he said. 'Perry, let's get this jalopy on the move.'

Peregrene had the engine running already, and as the doors slammed shut he wrenched the ageing car into gear and sent it surging down the gravelled lane. Two soldiers appeared beside a giant cactus plant, dropped to a prone position and levelled rifles towards the car. They were a second or two too late.

The route to the airport led more or less through the centre of Vanna; it made speed difficult and dangerous. The Citroen swayed round corners and streaked through the narrow streets, bordered by run-down houses and shops. There was an ugly moment when a hen flapped into the road, then bounced off the front of the car in a mass of flying feathers and blood spatters, which dotted the windscreen like coloured rain. 'Damn, damn, damn!' muttered Perry, pushing the accelerator pedal hard down to the floor.

A road joined the route, coming obliquely in from the right. Charlie glanced quickly along it. 'Hell!' he said. 'That's done it, mate. There's an army lorry up there. It's clocking about a hundred.'

'Keep watching it,' said Perry. They hurtled on, the car rattling and squeaking over the bumps, and thudding ominously from underneath.

Jonathan felt that choking sense of fear again. 'Have we anything to stop them with?' he croaked. 'Any guns?'

'No guns,' said Perry tersely. 'Just brains. Watch that army truck.'

'He's right behind us,' said Charlie, 'and really moving.'

'How far behind?'

'Half a mile. Maybe three-quarters.'

'Is he gaining?'

'I don't think so. But he's holding us. He'll probably open fire in a minute.'

'Yeah.'

'Got any plans?'

Most of the built-up area was behind them now. The road grew narrower than ever – only the centre of it was metalled, and then just to a single car's width. On each side were deeply rutted shoulders, rough enough to throw the old Citroen irrecoverably out of control. Perry was steering with the delicacy of a Grand Prix driver, measuring his position down to inches. 'We've gotta get rid of that truck,' he said. 'That's all I know.'

'What'll I do – spit at it?' asked Charlie.

They hit about eleven large potholes with axle-breaking force, and Jonathan felt the rear of the car begin to slew away to the left. A new wave of panic gripped him. Instinctively, he put his hands on the top of his head to protect it from the agonizing violence of the finish, and closed his eyes. Then, when he looked again, the car was back under control and hurtling on down the centre of the road. He ran the tip of his tongue round his lips, and took his hands down from his head.

'I'm surprised they haven't started shooting yet,' said Charlie.

'Work it out. They reckon they'll get us easier at the airport.'

'Yeah. That makes sense.'

'Now listen, all of you,' said Perry still in that drawly voice, but emphasizing every word. 'We're not far from the airport, and I'm going to abandon the car. You're to do exactly what I say the moment I say it.'

Wally spoke her first words of the journey. 'I can't walk another step,' she said. 'And that's flat.'

Charlie turned round, a flash of anger in his eyes. 'You shut up!' he said. And for once, Wally took it from him.

The road curved away, now, to the right.

'Is that truck still as far behind?' asked Peregrene. Charlie had a quick look. 'Yuh.'

'Right, well, this is it. I'm pulling off the road behind that hovel.' He pointed towards a decayed, red, single-storey building, probably a shepherd's simple shelter, standing just beyond the bend in the road.

Perry clamped his foot on the brake, and the car dipped its nose as the well-worn Michelins gripped at the road, and slipped, and gripped again, and slipped; he hauled the wheel round, and the Citroen swung right, rolling on its suspension system until even at this late stage it seemed they might capsize. Then the car stopped.

Perry shut off the engine. 'Everybody out!' he yelled. 'Get round to the front. Quick!'

They could hear the hum of the approaching truck, and every second the sound grew louder. A slight slope to the ground beside the hovel set the Citroen moving slowly backwards as Wally struggled out. Peregrene chocked the left, front wheel by jamming a foot behind it. 'Get a move on,' he shouted. 'Charlie, help her.' But before Charlie could do it, Wally hauled herself proudly out and glared at him defiantly.

'Go on, then, all of you. Round to the front, and when I say push – *push*, and don't go beyond the front of the hut.' Perry was at his best; very cool, thinking well ahead, absolutely in control.

The truck was close now, clattering round the bend, its engine screaming in third gear.

'All right – push!' yelled Perry, taking his foot away from the wheel. *'Hard!'* The old Citroen began to roll backwards into the narrow road. 'Harder, for Pete's sake!' The car picked up speed. Charlie was grunting with the effort.

'Now, all let go – *and stand back.*' The car carried on by itself across the road.

What happened in the next few seconds shocked Jonathan to the point where he lost the power to move. All he could do was stand, and look and soak in dreadful pictures of men and things arcing through the air, hear the tearing of metal, and suffer with the Citroen as the army truck mounted it at enormous speed, crushed it, rolled it, picked it up like one giant insect devouring another, and somersaulted down the road with it still in an inseparable embrace. The noise and motion stopped at last. Jonathan stood rooted and pale, staring at the wreckage, and at the remains of a shattered eucalyptus tree poking out between the chassis

of the truck and the broken crank-case of the car.
Liquids began to gurgle and splash about, and then to
trickle thinly along the metalled surface of the road.
There was oil, hot water, blood.

Wally was moaning quietly in the background. 'Oh

dear, oh dear,' she said. 'What a terrible thing. Terrible thing. Somebody help those men. Oh dear me,
dear me.'

Even Charlie was looking stunned. Tasma had
turned away preferring the sight of the barren countryside behind them.

Peregrene spoke first. 'Let's get on to the airport,'
he said. 'D'you all hear me? Jonathan – come on.'

But the boy stayed where he was, immobile.

'Jonathan!' Perry's voice had sharpened now. 'Come on, Jonno. We've gotta get going.'

'What do we do about the men?' asked Charlie. 'Just leave them?'

'That's right. There's nothing we can do for them. Come on.'

Daylight was fading quickly as they staggered on to the field and towards Yankee Foxtrot. A little car had been parked near by, and Colonel Moukef was standing leaning against the fuselage talking to Roz, who'd perched herself on the wing root. She waved excitedly when she suddenly saw the others coming. 'Hullo,' she called. 'Great. You've done it. You're all there – Wally too. Heavens! You seem to have got another one.' She hopped down from the wing.

'I'm Tasma,' said Tasma simply. 'Jonathan's friend.' She was mocking him a little.

'Er, yes,' agreed Jonathan. 'She helped us get out, and now she's coming with us.'

The Colonel hardly bothered to look at Tasma. He had a knowing and satisfied smile on his face which he pointed towards Perry. 'So!' he said. 'No problems then? Good, very good. Just as the King and I predicted.'

For a moment, Perry looked at the man as if he'd been speaking Chinese. 'A shambles,' he answered at last. 'That's what it's been. A goddam shambles! But I guess we're here – somehow. Look, let's get Yankee Foxtrot fired up and go. Colonel, there are some soldiers back there who need attention. They crashed while chasing us. I'm real sorry they had to get hurt.'

Moukef squeezed his lips together expressively. 'Soldiers are expendable,' he said blandly. 'Good-bye.'

He shook hands formally with the men and with Jonathan, bowed to the ladies, and then with both hands waved them all towards the aircraft. 'Be quick, please,' he said. 'There will be more soldiers soon. I would prefer us all to be gone by the time they arrive.'

Despite her breathlessness and ridiculous harem clothes, Wally made a big effort to switch on a show of dignity. She fixed Moukef with her deep set little eyes and spoke some parting words in a quavery voice. 'I can't say my visit to Mambay has been a pleasure,' she said. 'But it has been *most* worth while. All my fears were fully realized. *Fully.* I shall be reporting everything – *everything* to Sir William on my return. You may be sure swift action will follow. Oh yes, yes, I'm far from being finished with Youssef.'

Charlie scowled at her. 'Get in the ruddy aeroplane,' he said. 'We'll have the speeches later.'

Suddenly, Roz threw something towards Jonno. 'Catch,' she said, and to the boy's delight, he found himself holding his shorts in his hands. 'Gosh, thanks Roz,' he muttered. 'I'm glad to see these again.' He hopped behind Yankee Foxtrot's fuselage and changed into them as the others started to clamber aboard.

Just as Wally was about to start the struggle with Charlie to get up on to the wing, she turned towards him and slapped him vigorously on the shoulder. 'And where are my things, then?' she demanded. 'My clothes and suitcase. And my hat?'

'Under the army truck,' answered Charlie. 'In the back end of the Citroen.'

'Well, really. Outrageous! Absolutely outrage—'

Charlie cut her short. 'Go on, *hup*,' he said, heaving her on to the wing root, 'and keep your feet on the black bit for once,' he added.

There were six of them this time – a full house. Perry sat front left, Charlie beside him. Then, in the middle row, came Tasma, left, and Jonno, right. Behind the boy sat Roz. And tucked safely into the back left-hand corner was Wally; she raved on to Roz about the loss of her things. Mostly it was the hat she seemed to care about. 'Fifty years,' she kept saying. 'Fifty years I've had it.' Roz made soothing sounds and patted her knee, and waited for the storm to pass.

As usual, it was a huge thrill to Jonathan to be back in the comfortable inside of Yankee Foxtrot. He adored the solid old Aztec B – everything about it including the smell, a subtle mixture of upholstery, fuel, lubricating oil and lord knows what else.

Peregrene and Charlie got briskly down to the start-up routines. Master switch on, mixture rich, prime left then right, fine pitch, throttles cracked open, then start left, then right. Soon the engines were thrumming away, the aircraft trembling – as eager, one would have thought, as the people inside her to be off and heading for home; to Lonehead, and the good and familiar things that waited there.

Jonno listened to the engines and closed his eyes with pleasure and relief.

When the oil had warmed and thinned, they ran up the engines tumultuously, one then the other, and checked mags, sending a cloud of red dust billowing back behind them. Through the half light, they saw Moukef's little car drive away.

'What about lights?' asked Charlie. 'On or off?'

'All on, as we start to roll. Landing lights too.'

'Right. Everything on.'

Perry ran through the pre-take-off 'vital actions': trim to neutral, throttle friction up a bit, mixture rich,

111

carb heat cold, pitch fine, fuel booster pumps on, flap – 10 degrees, hatches secure and harness tight. He turned his head and glanced round the cabin. 'Is everything okay? Belts tight? Jonathan, how about yours?'

'Tight, Perry.'

'And what about ma'am back there? Roz, is her belt tight?'

Roz checked quickly and confirmed.

'Right, that's it. Let's go. Charlie, lights on, and stand by to raise the gear.'

'Roger, mate.' Charlie switched on the lights and a broad arc of yellowness spread out like a luminous carpet in front of them. The Lycomings came up to full power and the brakes went off. Yankee Foxtrot began to roll, gathering speed and bumping on the roughly laid runway. Jonathan, leaning forward as far as the belt would allow studied the glowing panel in front of him. All engine instruments were nicely in the green, and the air-speed indicator was swinging round the dial. Early in the take-off run, the stick moved firmly backwards and Yankee Foxtrot put her tail down a little, easing the load on the drubbing nosewheel. At that moment he smiled, an involuntary smile, small but lingering – just a deflection at the corners of his mouth which gave away his feelings. They'd done it – got away with it again. Something more to talk about – with proper modesty of course – for the whole of the rest of his flipping life.

At about 50 knots the heavy thumping from the main wheels faded as the weight came off them. A couple of seconds more and Yankee Foxtrot would be where she fitted best; in the air.

Jonathan glanced up ahead, across the yellow carpet of light towards the distant edge of the airfield. Then came a surprise. There was something there, ahead of them, in the way. A man – surely it was. No, perhaps a shadow. But you could see the whitish patch of his face. So it was a man, must be a man, and he was standing there, right in the path and looking towards them. The smile vanished from the boy's lips, and a prickle of fear went through him.

'Look!' The word came out as a husky croak. He tried again, yelled it this time. '*Look!* We'll hit him.'

The man showed up better now, floodlit by Yankee Foxtrot's advancing lights. Charlie lunged forward, straining to see through the screen. 'Keep going!' he shouted. 'Just keep her rolling.'

Perry had seen the figure just about at the moment when Jonno gave his warning croak. Like the boy, he thought for a moment he was seeing something that wasn't there. Then he was sure, quite sure, and instinctively began to shut off the power – then slammed the throttles open again. Why not? The guy was standing there from his own choice. He could see them coming. It was up to him to duck – or die.

They were very close now, and just starting to lift away. The man had a chunk of something in his hand, and was drawing his arm back like an outfielder about to make a long, well-aimed throw. You could see him clearly now. A tall gaunt figure, bespectacled, very erect, dressed in the dark clothes of a city broker and capped by a strong growth of bright white hair blowing loosely in the evening breeze.

Jonathan's sharp eyes identified him fractionally sooner than Peregrene and Charlie. The croak was back again as he called the name: 'It's Sir William Krier, Sir William . . . !'

The man's arm jerked forward – the action that goes

with throwing a spear – and the shape he'd been holding left his hand and flew towards Yankee Foxtrot,
homing on to the starboard side. In the less than a
second that the shape took to complete its flight, the
three of them saw what it was: A large and heavy
lump of reddish-grey rock.

With the roaring Aztec almost on top of him, the
man flung himself down in a brutal bellyflop on to
the ground, and covered his head with his arm.

Chapter Six

STRUGGLE FOR HEIGHT

The impact of the rock as it crashed into Yankee Foxtrot's polished alloy starboard propeller running on
full power was appalling.

First came an enormous bang, so loud a bang that it
numbed the mind and felt like a physical assault on the
inner ear. Then came more bangs, a lot of them, fast
and repeating and varying in loudness – a sound-effect
that lay somewhere between machine-gun fire and the
clatter of shrapnel landing on metal surfaces.

Charlie threw a hand up to the right side of his face
at the same moment as a piece of rock smashed through
the perspex window and hit him agonizingly on the
knuckles and backs of his fingers. 'Oh God, my hand!'
he yelled, putting it under his left arm for comfort
and protection, and crouching forward in pain. A
massive suction centred now on the shattered window
sending strong currents of air vortexing round the
cabin.

Jonathan, sitting stunned by the suddenness of the
calamity heard Perry shouting to Charlie. 'Feather,
feather,' he was calling. 'Quick, man.' But Charlie,
obsessed for the moment with the pain of his injured
hand, was slow to react. Peregrene, fighting for control
of the aircraft, began to do the feathering drill himself.
A furious vibration had set up in the starboard engine
nacelle and was growing worse – the sort of violence

that can tear engines out of their mountings or rip a wing clean away from the fuselage.

Jonathan found words at last. 'I'll feather,' he called, snapping loose his seatbelt and leaning forward between the two men. Perry had already closed the starboard throttle. Now Jonathan pulled back the green knob of the pitch control, then put the mixture lever to lean. The propeller, the twisted ruin that was left of it, stopped turning.

They were flying on full left rudder, the port engine bellowing away on full power and fine pitch. It looked as if they were hardly more than a hand's-width above the ground, and Perry was easing off the flap, very slowly, very carefully, afraid of the little bit of sink that would have them tearing the bottom out of Yankee Foxtrot in an unintentional wheels-up landing. He was struggling to maintain 90 knots, the minimum single-engine climb speed. Slightly more than 90 was showing on the clock and they began to gain height, just a foot or two, and with every foot counting.

'Light off,' ordered Peregrene – and Jonathan switched it off.

Charlie took his hand out from his armpit, and glanced at it. There was blood there, and the whole hand had puffed up and was turning purple. Jonno squeezed his shoulder sympathetically.

Yankee Foxtrot began to win the struggle for height. When the altimeter showed a hundred feet, Jonathan felt like cheering loudly. Instead, he offered a word or two of praise to Captain Langhorne.

'Well done, Perry,' he said. 'That's great – we've got a hundred on the clock now.'

Peregrene looked so cool he might have been sitting at a movie show, but he was working very hard, his eyes everywhere, searching the panel and skyline, his sensitive hands willing the old aircraft upwards. Perry was putting all he had into the delicate task of keeping Yankee Foxtrot and her heavy load in flight.

With the extra speed, the inside draughts were growing stronger and picking up dust from the floor which blew irritatingly into everyone's eyes. Jonathan turned to see how the rear-seat passengers were making out. Roz looked rather pale, but smiled valiantly, and he smiled back.

'You okay, then?' he asked.

'Yes, thanks, Jonno. Fine.'

'Good. Blimey! Look at her.'

Wally had thrown her head back and half closed her eyes. Her prim-looking mouth sagged open. 'I know what she's doing,' the boy went on. 'She's wake-sleeping again. Oh blimey, what a sight.'

'Be quiet,' said Wally without opening her eyes, and sounding oddly detached, as if she might be speaking from a distant cloud. 'You're disturbing me.'

'I'm sorr*ee*,' he replied, looking to the front. 'So sorr*ee*' – then, in an undertone – 'I don't think.'

Wally hadn't been supposed to hear the last words against the roar of the engine, but of course she did. 'That's impertinent,' she snapped. 'Stop it.'

Jonathan reddened slightly in the darkness. He could sense Tasma grinning beside him, but pretended not to notice.

Half a minute or so later, Perry turned to peer past Charlie towards the starboard wing. Jonathan was aware of something new and strange about the attitude of the aircraft; looking at the turn and bank indicator, he decided they were skidding left with the right wing low – the dangerous beginnings of a spiral dive.

Charlie had more or less recovered now, although

his right hand was clearly useless. 'What's on?' he asked Perry.

'That wing,' replied Perry tersely, staring past him. 'What's it doing?'

Charlie looked intently. 'Hell, yes. We've got more trouble, mate. There's a lump of metal skin off the top. It's sticking up into the airstream.'

Fear came back to Jonathan. One emotion seemed to chase another all the time – as soon as one danger passed and relief could set in, another took its place. Surely they weren't going to crash now – not now, after all they'd gone through. He looked again at the altimeter. Gosh, they were down to 80 feet. Fear grew quickly, overwhelmingly, like an ice-cold blanket wrapped round him, wrapped so tightly he couldn't move and could barely breathe.

Perry spoke again. 'I can't maintain height. What d'you make of it, Charlie?'

'I think we've had it, mate.' Charlie peered along the wing again. 'I think it's getting worse. It's slowly peeling off.'

Perry switched the landing lights on again. 'Everybody listen,' he said. His voice was quiet, but clear and authoritative. 'We're gonna crash land. Get those belts good and tight. Put your arms over your faces. All keep quiet.'

With trembling fingers, Jonno put his belt back on and pulled it tight. Tasma reached over and squeezed his hand. He managed to squeeze hers back, then they both covered their faces and waited.

Perry had the port throttle partly closed now, and Yankee Foxtrot was flying straighter, but losing height quite quickly. 'I'm gonna want full flap in a second or so, Charlie,' he said. 'Okay?'

'Yes. Okay. It's darned hard to see much in front there. What're you going to do?'

'I'm just going in dead ahead. We can't choose. Listen, when I say *off* – I want all the works off. You with me?'

'Sure. Fuel cocks, mags, master – everything off.'

'Right.'

'Gear up?'

'Yeah. Gear up. Okay, full flap – *now*.'

'Roger, mate. Good luck.' Charlie pushed the flap lever down and Yankee Foxtrot began to try to raise her nose. Instantly, Perry took the forward pressure on the stick and pointed her downwards, towards the ground, losing speed. Altitude was falling away fast. Perry shut the power right off, and brought the speed back to 65 knots. They were almost at ground level now, and rocks and stubby trees were flashing dimly past. The stick came further and further back, and the Aztec pointed her nose slowly higher towards the stall position.

'Off!' called Perry – and with his left hand, Charlie snapped the cocks and switches off. The lights went out and the engine cut dead. You could hear the wind whistling past the broken window. Then a scraping sound from the rear told that the tail had touched down. A sudden brief sensation of sinking followed – then a violent buffeting and rising crescendo of noise as old Yankee Foxtrot had the bottom largely ripped out of her fuselage, chunk by chunk.

Jonno felt himself being shaken and jarred and vibrated. Soon, out of the side of his eye, he saw the wingtip on his side smash into a dark mass of something, and the aircraft swung viciously to the right and his forearms and head crashed forward on to the back of Charlie's seat jerking his neck back with a sharpness that he feared might have broken it.

At last the motion stopped and there seemed nothing but silence and darkness left in the world. Then a few groans and gasps began and Wally gave a single, shuddering sob. Jonathan turned his head painfully to look at her. She was streaming with blood from her

nose. Roz had her head buried in her hands and seemed to be weeping silently. Tasma's hair had sprung forward over her face, and she was staring through it, rubbing her right forearm and sighing with pain. He looked to the front now. Perry seemed to have been stunned and was drooped across the control column. In the right-hand seat, Charlie was rubbing his neck with his one good hand, and swearing softly.

Despite his own misery, Jonathan felt a surge of concern for Peregrene. 'Charlie,' he whispered. 'Look at Perry – he's hurt.'

Charlie stopped swearing. 'Yeah,' he said and, undoing his seatbelt leaned over to make a diagnosis. Perry seemed to see him and mumbled something incoherent. 'Wha . . . wha,' he said.

Slowly, Charlie turned round and studied the others. 'Perry's concussed a bit,' he said. 'Come to think of it, nobody's looking very good. What a mess. Look, Jonno, we'd better get everyone out of here. We might still catch fire.'

One of Perry's feet had jammed under the rudder pedal and Charlie had a struggle to free him and lift him clear of the aircraft. Then, one by one, they staggered out through the door and sat, dazed and bruised, on the hard red ground.

Roz crawled over to look at Perry lying stretched out on his back. She passed near Tasma on the way, and paused there. 'See if you can help Mrs Kidwallader Jones,' she whispered, then crept on. When she reached him, she gazed down with fondness and concern at his lean, weathered face, then touched his brow. Putting her mouth close to his ear, she murmured his name. 'Perry,' she said. 'Oh Perry.'

And after a moment, Peregrene answered. He turned his head a little to see her. 'Hi, Roz,' he said dreamily. 'What's been going on here?'

She looked radiant now, and quite beautiful, a broad smile taking control of her smudged yet still elegant face. 'Perry! You're all right, then. Oh, how wonderful.' She lowered her head on to his chest and could feel his heart beating, a strong, slow beat.

'We crash-landed,' she murmured on. 'You did it. A super job. And we're all alive.'

Soon she moved her head away, and Perry sat up to stare at the wreckage of Yankee Foxtrot. 'Yes, yes, I remember now. That guy and the rock. What the hell did he do it for? Poor old Yankee Foxtrot. It doesn't look as if she'll ever fly again. Charlie – are you all right?'

'Most of me is, mate. I've busted my right hand.'

'And you Jonno?'

'Yes, Perry. My neck hurts, that's all. Well, and my arm a bit.'

'What about old Wally, there? She seems rough.'

Roz answered: 'She hit her nose, poor thing. She's not too bad though. We're all okay, really. Very lucky we are – but we did choose a good pilot.'

'Yeah, that's right. So you did.' He smiled.

'Look,' said Tasma suddenly. 'Over there. Lights.'

They all looked, in silence. There were headlights in the distance; three pairs of them, and drawing closer.

Jonathan put the obvious question. 'Who d'you think it is? Colonel Moukef? Or' – the tone of his voice changed – 'or Youssef?'

Perry pulled himself slowly on to his feet. 'I don't know,' he said, sounding very matter of fact. 'Could be either. My God, but my head aches.'

The leading car arrived in a swirl of dust, its headlights glaring into their eyes. Four armed soldiers sprang out and began shouting excitedly in Arabic. They gestured at the group to move closer to each other, waving pistols at them to drive the message home.

Wally began to shout hysterically. 'I just can't bear any more of it,' she screeched. 'I demand to be released. Somebody tell them. Tell them to let us go. *Tell them!*'

Roz shook her head towards the poor, fat, tired and

ageing Wally. 'Try to keep calm,' she said. 'Please!'

Two other cars slithered to a stop on the loose surface and, with their arrival, the glare intensified, and the shouting grew more confused and frightening.

'Tasma,' said Roz, through the uproar. 'Can you make anything out of what they're saying?'

'Not much. Only that we're all arrested.'

One soldier who seemed to be in charge walked up to Tasma, put his face close to hers, and screamed an unintelligible order. 'I think they mean be quiet,' said Perry. Then the soldier walked up to him and screamed again, prodding away at his chest with a stubby finger. That seemed to confirm it. So they stood in anguished silence.

The soldier walked over to the lead car which carried a radio, and took out a microphone. They could see him talking into it.

A long wait began, with Wally swaying about on her feet looking exhausted to the point of collapse. Jonathan felt a tear trickle down his cheek, to be followed by another, and another. A soldier came up to him and began to laugh and point, and then other soldiers gathered to mock and torment him. Then one who'd had a cruel grin on his face wiped the grin away, and came up so close that Jonathan could smell the stale, hot breath. The boy moved his head away, and at that moment the soldier's hand came swiftly up to strike him a stunning slap on the left cheek. It was Jonathan's turn to sway for a moment, and a flood of tears rolled down his face now from the pain of the blow – but the flood was short lived. A wave of passionate anger swept through him and banished the tears leaving him pale, intense and in control of himself.

At last an army lorry drove up, and they were all

forced into it with two soldiers for company. The cars formed up as an escort, one in front and two in line astern formation behind, and the convoy set off at speed.

They juddered and rocked their way back into central Vanna with Wally groaning at every rut and ridge and pothole the stiffly sprung lorry clattered over. Wearily, Jonno noticed they were driving parallel to a huge, defensive wall, and through gardens he had last seen when walking with Sergeant Houmman to the harem. So now he knew. It was Youssef's place they were going to. Lord knows what waited for them there.

The lorry slowed down to pass through the checkpoints, and stopped eventually in the floodlit courtyard, parked close up to the main entrance of Youssef's enormous house. Soldiers began to swarm round the tailgate like agitated ants, and grabbed at the prisoners' hands and ankles hauling them all roughly out.

They were escorted into a spacious office with whitewashed walls and a tiled floor. A vast sienna-coloured desk stood at the end of the room in front of a second doorway. At the desk, like a uniformed bull, sat Youssef; sitting beside him, and dwarfed by the other man's colossal size, was Sir William Krier.

On the front of Sir William's expensive suit were patches of red dust. Wally, clinging to Roz and Tasma for support, quivered at the sight of him. Her eyes, red-rimmed and peering now from above big, dark bags of tiredness, looked on to the bland face and silvery hair. A gasp came out of her, carried away on a long, slow exhalation of air. Then she found breath for a single, venomously uttered word: 'Traitor!' She hissed it out, and began to shake so violently that it occurred to Jonathan that she might be having a fit. Roz and Tasma tightened their hold on her, but dared not speak.

*

A tall van creaked up in the darkness of the north wall of Youssef's grounds, and parked there. In the back sat ten keyed-up soldiers. They were all armed – nine with automatic pistols, the tenth with an old but immaculate Sten gun. A vertical ladder had been screwed to the inside of the van, and led up to a square hole cut in the roof.

The driver wore a plain civilian djelaba top garment. On the right of the cab sat a young, thin-faced, earnest-looking army officer. In the middle, between the officer and driver, showing a little fixed smile, and turning his head from side to side like an eager terrier sniffing out a rabbit, sat King Abdellah.

As the van stopped, Yacoub gripped his father's arm. 'Now listen, Father,' he said to the King. 'As soon as we're over the wall, get away from here and find Moukef by the fig trees. Follow him up the tunnel and we'll meet inside. And one thing more, Father, by the Lord of the Glorious Throne – don't get caught.' He climbed down from the cab, nipped round to the back and got in with the soldiers.

A coiled rope ending in a U-shaped piece of metal lay on the floor. Yacoub slung it over his shoulder, went quickly up the ladder and pulled himself on to the wall. Lying there, flat, he inverted the U-piece like a hat on the wall's top, and lowered the rope to dangle inside the grounds.

'Come on,' he whispered through the hole in the roof. 'Follow me, and be quiet and quick. Bring the

125

bag of tools.' Hand over hand he went down the rope to the coarse grass on the inside. The men followed him, up the ladder and down the rope. One of them brought the heavy holdall of tools. Keeping close to the wall, they gathered opposite the entrance to Youssef's harem.

'Now, have your guns ready,' ordered Yacoub. 'But remember, I don't want anyone shot if we can avoid it. And we should be able to avoid it.' They sped silently across the grass, then on tip-toe across the metalled roadway to arrive at the solid front door of the harem. Yacoub rang the bell, a long, hard ring.

At last the door opened and a sleepy eunuch stood before them. He had a gun in his hand. Yacoub moved with a panther's speed and knocked the gun from the man's hand with a karate chop across the wrist. In rapid Arabic he warned the panicking eunuch to be quiet. They crowded in through the hallway, then, when everyone was safely in, softly closed the front door. Yacoub calmed the trembling guard, promising not to hurt him providing he behaved. Then he turned to his own men. 'Take your boots off,' he said. 'Leave them here.'

The women and other eunuchs were asleep, which made the rest of the invasion easy. They simply left the women to slumber on, and tackled the eunuchs in stealthy silence, one at a time, trussing them up like plump chickens. On one of the guards they found a key, which Yacoub took over to the closed trapdoor. It fitted, as he'd been sure it would, and he unlocked the door and swung it down. Crouched above the opening a smile on his lean face, Yacoub heard approaching movements from below. Soon his father appeared up the ladder, beaming and turning his head pertly, this way and that, like an eccentric jack-in-the-box. Moukef and four soldiers followed behind.

Yacoub put a warning finger to his lips. 'Shsh,' he whispered. 'Please – not a sound.'

The King looked round the great room. He was clearly feeling pleased with himself. 'You've had no trouble I see,' he murmured, 'just as Moukef and I thought.'

'Shsh,' whispered Yacoub again, anxiously. 'It isn't over yet, Father. In fact, we've barely begun. Take your shoes off please – everyone.'

Yacoub selected a small squad from the men and, with Moukef beside him and the King tottering along at the back, made his way to Youssef's private room at the rear of the harem. The room abutted the main part of the house, but there was no connecting doorway. Laboriously, using padded hammers and a huge jemmy, the soldiers pulled away at chunks of masonry until there was a big enough opening for them all to climb through.

*

The uniformed bull pounded his desk top three or four times with the flats of his powerful hands, and shouted with laughter. Turning, he thumped Sir William next, and thumped him so hard he slightly dislodged the Englishman's spectacles. 'Go on, Bill,' he jested, 'have a laugh at that lot. What a sight, eh? And you know something? – that fat one's a woman of mine. She's escaped from my palace. By the Prophet, she'll be punished for that.' The smile dissolved without warning into a scowl, and he half rose from his chair, frowning at Wally. 'How the hell did you get out of there?' he demanded in a voice harsh with fury. 'I'll have you beaten for that – I'll flay you to pulp.'

But Wally was too far gone with the shakes to react.

Sir William placed a thin, white hand on the big man's sleeve. 'No, Youssef,' he said. 'We're past the beatings stage. They must be executed, all of them, right away – the child, too. If anyone of them escapes – well, you know what the consequences will be.'

'Consequences?' Youssef swivelled his cold, tyrant's eyes back to Sir William. 'For you, perhaps,' he went on. 'There'll be no consequences for me, Billy Krier – none. So, don't think there will be.'

Sir William smiled coolly. 'I think you might miss my advice a little, Youssef – don't you? You're a good soldier I know, but be honest – you're hardly a brain.'

A pause followed, then Youssef grinned, showing crooked, oddly white teeth. 'We might as well get rid of them I suppose,' he said. 'I'll have them shot. That's easiest.'

'When?'

'Now. I'll get the guard out.' He turned to the stricken group. 'You hear that, you lot?' he asked. He was grinning again, looking them over one by one. 'You're going to be shot tonight. Make the best of the next few minutes.' The grin grew in size and ugliness and converted itself at last into snorting laughter.

Jonno's entire inside seemed to turn to ice-cold liquid. He felt sick and began to sway dizzily on his feet. Then Charlie moved softly up from behind to stand beside him, and took his hand and held it. The boy turned, and lowered his head to rest it against the comforting arm, and waited, his eyes closed, praying for the nausea to pass. He heard Youssef shouting in Arabic, then there were answering shouts and more laughter, from behind this time – from the soldiers.

They seemed to enjoy the thought of a mass execution.

What happened next, happened fast. First, Jonathan felt Charlie stiffen and hiss a little air through his teeth. Then came a loud crash from beyond Youssef's desk. And an instant after that, something exploded at the back of the room.

Jonno jerked his head up and looked. A young, strongly-built man in a khaki shirt with military-style pips on his shoulder tabs, was standing inside Youssef's private door, which had been flung back against the wall. He was pointing a pistol at the big man's head. And beyond the doorway, Jonathan caught a quick glimpse of something that surprised him greatly. It was the King himself. King Abdellah, the bookworm, and he was smiling.

The young man spoke. 'Don't move a muscle, Youssef,' he said, 'or you'll never move again.' Youssef knew, everybody knew, that the young man meant it.

Chapter Seven

HIT ME HERE

Jonathan looked behind him to see the soldiers – seven of them – who'd been in such jeering good spirits a moment before, backing apprehensively into the far corner of the room; two were holding their hands in the air at shoulder height.

Crouched in the main doorway, and pointing a sub-machine-gun towards them all, was Moukef. He had a cocky little smile on his lips. Several large lumps had been knocked out of the walling facing him, and thin discs of smoke were drifting slowly about the room.

Jonathan realized now what the explosion had been – a short burst of fire; an instant message to the men, and one which they had obviously understood. Then Moukef said something in Arabic, keeping his voice low and controlled. One by one the soldiers put their pistols on to the floor, dabbed at them with a foot and sent them sliding across the tiles out of reach.

Perry had turned round, too, and drawled a few words of relief. 'It's a real pleasure to see you, Colonel,' he said.

'Yeah,' added Charlie. 'It was the right time to call.'

Moukef nodded, keeping his eyes alertly fixed on the soldiers. 'Thank you, gentlemen,' he said. 'Please help yourselves to a gun. Jonathan, too.'

They stepped forward, followed by Tasma. 'I'll have one as well,' she said. 'I'm a very good shot.' She picked the thing up, checked it over coolly, moved the safety catch to off and casually fired a shot through the window. The bang was so loud it made Jonathan jump.

Outwardly at least, Youssef made a quick recovery from the shocks he'd just had. He banged the desk top again. 'Yacoub,' he said. 'You should have let me know you were coming. I'd have had a proper welcome for you.' He put his head back and laughed. Sir William seemed to be making an effort to keep up and showed his teeth in a quivering smile; he'd gone very white in the face.

'Get up, Youssef,' ordered Yacoub, gesturing with the gun.

The big man stared steadily back at Yacoub. 'Look, boy,' he said. 'If you're going to shoot me, go ahead and shoot now. I'd rather have it sitting down.' He turned to put his bull chest squarely facing the gun. 'Come close,' he added. 'Hit me here, in the heart. I don't want it in the gut or up my nose. Got it, boy? I want it here.' He put one huge hand – his left – over his heart, and beckoned Yacoub towards him with the other.

But Yacoub made no move. 'You're not going to be shot, Youssef,' he said evenly. 'Not if you behave. You're going to write a letter to my father resigning all the state offices you hold. You're going round with me to speak to the higher ranks in the army to tell them they owe their allegiance now to the King. Then, in the morning, we're going to parade the entire army and you're going to stand in front where everyone can see you while we strip you publicly of your ranks and medals. After which, you're going straight out of the country and you're never coming back. Have you followed that?'

Youssef took in the message, then he began to rock his heavy shoulders with loud laughter again. 'You mean you're not going to kill me?' he yelled. 'Is that right?'

'Yes. You heard me. Killing isn't our way.'

Youssef guffawed again, and smashed his hands on to the desk top. Then, suddenly. the shouts of laughter and the shaking stopped. 'You haven't the guts, Yacoub! Have you, boy?' he said.

The expression on Yacoub's dark face changed. 'Sit very still, Youssef,' he said. 'Stiller than you've ever sat before.' He raised the pistol towards the ceiling, straightened his arm, then lowered away slowly. Sir William, watching the muzzle of the gun come creeping down to point at Youssef alongside him, sprang from his chair and pressed back against the wall.

Absolute silence came to the roomful of people watching, and then, after a three- or four-second pause, Yacoub squeezed the trigger. Another deafening bang sounded, and something flew from Youssef's left shoulder.

'That's one we won't have to rip off you,' said Yacoub.

Youssef grabbed at the shoulder with his right hand, and swore. When he looked at his fingers there was some blood there, but not much. No more than would come from a deepish scratch.

'Good shot!' said a reedy voice from the other end of the room. King Abdellah had shown himself. 'Ah, Rosemary-Anne,' he went on, seeing her with pleasure, 'I hope you're not harmed.'

'No, Your Majesty. Not in the least. But can we have a chair for Mrs Kidwallader Jones, please? She's just in a state of collapse.' .

'Yes, of course, of course. We'll have to find one.
Youssef didn't believe in chairs for visitors, you see –
they had to kneel or something. Wait though, better
still, we'll all adjourn to his sitting room. It's very comfortable there. Moukef, attend to the men. Make them
swear their loyalty to me, and tell them I'm doubling
their pay. The rest of you – follow me.' He swept away
to the other room.

They helped Wally along the passage and stretched

her out on the richly upholstered couch. She was already almost unconscious on her feet; now she gave a long, resonant sigh and slipped into a sleep that looked likely to last for a week.

Sir William stood uneasily beside Youssef, who loomed over the King, now settled royally into a high-backed chair. The gun in Yacoub's hand remained pointed unwaveringly at the big man's head.

'Now, Yacoub,' said the King, 'get him to write the letter. After that, I want Moukef to parade my bodyguard, and we'll receive all the officers in the stateroom I think. They won't give us any trouble – take my word for it. Glad to be rid of this elephant I'm sure. Then I want him locked away in the cells for the night. That white-haired one, too.'

Sir William made one last play. He smiled unconvincingly and clasped his hands. 'Your Majesty,' he began, 'this is all a terrible mistake ... forty years in the city ... I do beg you to believe ...'

But King Abdellah waved him to silence. 'Take him to the cells at once,' he said. 'He's a bad one.'

In about fifteen minutes, Perry, Charlie, Jonathan, Roz and Tasma set off with the King for his palace, travelling in the royal car – a 37-year-old Rolls-Royce with oversize tyres. Wally was carried out on the couch by a party of sweating soldiers, and loaded into a van. She slept on through it all.

Nothing seemed to have changed at the run-down palace. The King led them through to his sitting room. 'A most satisfactory day,' he said. 'But I am sure you are all hungry, so Benahid will bring you food. You must excuse me if I retire now. It is very late, and tomorrow will be a busy time. The public parade will be at two o'clock. Then let us all dine together at six.'

He turned to smile quickly at Roz. 'My dear,' he murmured, 'you've seen Yacoub. He's, ah, how may I put it – a handsome young man, is he not?'

Roz worked very hard on the muscles of her lips and screwed out a smile in reply. 'Yes,' she agreed. 'He looks quite charming.'

The King chuckled with delight. 'And a crown prince – eh? That's rather nice, too? Anyway, you two will have a chance to get to know each other tomorrow. Good night to you, my dear – and, ah, to all of you.'

Still wearing a waspish little smile, King Abdellah trundled away to bed.

Twice Jonathan almost fell asleep while eating the fish and maize meal that Benahid's men carried in on the ready-laid table. Then he muttered good night to the others and lurched exhaustedly up to his room. The rest of them followed quite soon, and Charlie put his head round Jonathan's door to wish him no dreams or happy ones. But the boy was asleep, stretched out on his back, still wearing his shorts and nothing else, his dark hair matted with sweat and dust. An arm hung limply down to touch the floor.

Charlie lifted the arm up and placed it more comfortably on the bed, and walked off to his room. Moments later he was as soundly asleep himself.

Not much before eleven in the morning, Jonno woke up, and did so suddenly, rearing into a sitting position and searching the room with anxious eyes. Then he sank back again, grateful, and lay for a minute staring upwards while the swirl of tension receded. The dangers were over; yes, they were over now, and the sun was burning away at the palace again, forcing through the louvre shutters – a hundred slit-like flashlights. He picked his watch off the chair, but it had stopped. Anyway, he knew it must be getting late.

Everything seemed peaceful at the palace. He listened intently for a moment, but as far as he could hear nobody was moving in the other rooms. But blimey! What a night it had been. He rolled off his bed and padded through to Charlie's room.

Charlie was sitting on his bed, fully dressed, shaved and leaning against the wall with his hands clasped behind his head. 'Hi,' he said.

'Hullo, Charlie. What – what are you doing then?'

'Waiting for you. How're you feeling, Captain?'

Jonno smiled and walked over, and sat on the bed, too. 'Gosh, thanks, Charlie,' he said. 'I mean for waiting around.'

'Well, okay, but what about it then? *Are* you feeling all right?'

'Yes, now I am. Blimey, though. When I think about last night!'

Charlie sniffed. 'You pong a bit,' he said.

'Do I? I've been sweating a lot. I'd better have a wash.'

'Yeah. A good one. All the way.'

'Are the others up yet?'

'Yes, sir. You're last. We've had breakfast, and Perry's out having a look at Yankee Foxtrot.'

'What about the soldiers, and Youssef, and all that? I mean, is everything all right?'

'Yeah, under control. I hear Youssef's been snivelling in his cell all night.'

'Snivelling? Youssef?'

'Yes. Well, I don't think they've been too nice to him – some of the men he used to kick up the bum. That's life. Look, go ahead and have that wash. You remind me of a rubbish tip I once fell into near Hong Kong harbour.

'What about Tasma? Is she still here?'

'You bet. I think she's running the palace. Old Benahid's looking fidgety about it already. Wally's egging her on, too.'

'Oh, Wally! She's on the go again, is she?'

'My God. Don't ask. She's worse than ever. Jonno, for Peter's sake, have that flippin' wash. Do you hear all that chanting out there? Well, that's calling everyone to the big do this afternoon. I hear we've got ringside seats – part of the royal party and all that cods. So put on a shirt and some socks. Crikey, those shorts. Well, never mind, they'll do. If you get a move on, we can nip out for a look at the Aztec before the action starts.'

Jonathan, washed and cheerful, ate a bun and an orange as he and Charlie sped along the bumpy track towards Yankee Foxtrot in an army lorry, complete with driver, that Benahid had somehow supplied at an instant's notice. As they drew near, they saw the palace bus parked beside the wreckage, and Jonathan's mood changed. Perry was still there, moving slowly about, his hands in his pockets. Roz walked with him, her arm linked through his. A shimmy of heat rose from the sunbaked remains of Yankee Foxtrot's metal skin.

Jonno stepped out of the truck in dismayed amazement. There were bits of aircraft everywhere – dozens of bits, scattered widely around. Peregrene looked up as he and Charlie approached. 'Well, that's that,' he said. 'Good-bye to an airplane. She's done us okay, Charlie – until now.'

'Yep, she's done all right. And look over there, Perry. A wall of all things. A ruddy great wall out here, all by itself. We could have gone right through that, mate. We've been lucky.'

'Yeah, sure. Real lucky. We didn't even have a fire.'

But at that moment, Jonno couldn't see a single lucky aspect to the situation. With leaden heart, he picked his way through the pieces and stopped to read the big letters painted on the fuselage. G-ARYF. Golf Alpha Romeo Yankee Foxtrot. So that really was the end of Yankee Foxtrot. He ran a hand along the hot fuselage, then found a small piece of metal still bearing the orange and white livery of Peregrene's Western Aircharters Company – the colours he'd washed down so often. The metal lay, glinting, on the ground. He picked it up, and took it slowly over to Perry. 'Can I keep this, please?' he asked quietly. 'You know, a sort of a – of a – souvenir?'

Peregrene tapped him on the shoulder. 'Sure,' he said. 'But don't look so sad, Jonno. It's just an airplane. There are plenty of others in the world.'

'Thanks.'

Jonno turned back to the bus. He hadn't been fooled. Perry had a funny look on his face, too, and couldn't wholly conceal it.

*

The ceremony of the afternoon took place on a large piece of open ground adjoining the palace. Considering the short time there had been to arrange everything, it went off very well.

The King looked much bigger than his real size, sitting on a colourful, padded throne, and wearing purple and white robes with a jewelled headband glittering round the white *burnous* on his head; he was apparently quite untroubled by the heat. Yacoub stood beside him, standing stiffly to attention dressed in the uniform of a high-ranking officer – Jonathan

138

supposed it must be a general's gear. At least 500 men on snorting stallions stood along three sides of a square, facing inwards towards the King and leaving enough space between the horses' flanks for the ordinary people to see what was going on. Moukef was there, of course, with other officers, all arranged protectively round the royal pair.

About ten minutes later Youssef was brought to the square, surrounded by an eight-man escort armed with rifles. Jonathan, as one of the honoured guests, was sitting on a platform raised high enough for him to see the whole extraordinary spectacle. Could this great, shambling creature really be Youssef? What had changed? He still wore the uniform of yesterday, still carried the bull-like bulk of yesterday, standing a whole head taller than the tallest of his escorts. Yet the authority, the spark, the bounding pitiless soul of the man had gone.

The King reached for a microphone and harangued Youssef for almost 30 minutes in Arabic sentences that Jonathan reckoned might be heard as far away as Lonehead field. Loudspeakers were booming round the square and far beyond, right out among the great crowds of people. Every time the King paused for breath there were cheers and drummings from the distance.

Then came the terrible moment all the oratory and ceremonial had been leading towards. The King shouted a short sentence, and the bull knelt down. After a pause came another royal shout – and the crowd grew silent. With quick movements, the King's hands ripped chunks of uniform away, throwing them to the ground. They peeled from the cloth so easily it was obvious they had been half pulled off before.

Everything that mattered went. The shoulder tabs, scarlet flashes, the medals, leather belt, hat badge and buttons. Lastly came a slow, painful, utterly lonely stagger in the searing sun to an open lorry at the unlined end of the square.

Jonathan's last glimpse of Youssef was a rear one, as the broken bull drove at walking pace, in full view of the jeering crowd, on a long drive to the border.

'That's the end of him,' said Tasma brightly. 'Serves him right.'

'Yes,' said Jonathan. 'I suppose so.' He had funny feelings about the humiliation of a man though. Even of a thug of a man like Youssef.

'Did you understand what the King said?' went on Tasma.

'Of course not.'

'Well, I got some of it. He's going to hand over the throne to Yacoub quite soon, and lots of food and other things are going to be handed out in a feast tonight – they found tons of it at Youssef's house. There will be fireworks and dancing and I don't know what else besides. And you know something, I was talking to Yacoub this morning at breakfast.'

'You were?'

She nudged him hard. 'Yes, he's seen me. And he keeps looking. You know I've got some royal blood in me, do you? Well, a little. Come on, walk back to the palace with me.'

Jonathan threw a number of searching looks at Tasma as they strolled back to the palace ground. 'I think – d'you – I mean d'you mean you think Yacoub and you are going ... Look, I think King Abdellah wants Roz to, well, marry Yacoub or something.'

'Don't be silly,' said Tasma blandly. 'You just make

sure Roz goes home with you – or I'll have you back in the harem. And you know what as.'

A new, startling thought ran through Jonathan's mind about Tasma. Poor old King Abdellah had had his – what was it – his Fatima. Was Tasma going to be like that for Yacoub? Well, no. It just couldn't turn out like that again. Tasma was different – and sure as anything so was Yacoub.

*

The dinner party in the palace was on a bigger scale than anything they'd experienced there before. There were more than thirty guests, and among the people present was a chief superintendent from Scotland Yard who'd come for Sir William and was to fly him back next day. The evening finished with fireworks – a rich display of whirling, flaming colours.

When Jonathan went off at last for the night, Charlie and Perry both ambled into his room with him and saw him in to bed.

'What about all that, then, Jonno?' said Perry. 'It's ended pretty well – hasn't it? Not too badly, eh? We're flying home on an Air France Caravelle tomorrow. No work for us, Charlie, just champagne and air hostesses all the goddam way.'

Jonathan pulled a sheet up to his chin. 'Yes, but there's poor old Yankee Foxtrot,' he said. 'That's the awful part.'

'Ah, know what they're going to do with Yankee Foxtrot? They're going to put her together on a pedestal as a national memorial to Mambay's liberation from Youssef. She'll live for ever, floodlit too.'

Jonathan thought about it for a moment. 'That's not bad,' he said. 'Not bad at all. And we can come

141

back, just sometimes, to see her. Maybe sit inside her again.'

'Yeah,' said Charlie. 'And without old gasbag Wally. I like the thought of that.'

'Well, now, I'll just tell you another thing,' said Perry. 'Old Gasbag Wally has had something to do with all these cheering people out there. You'll have to admit that. And there's even more – she's going to buy us another airplane. So how d'you figure that?'

Charlie ran a hand through his reddish tangle of hair. 'Well,' he said, 'I've always been rather keen on the old girl really – in a secret sort of way. But, Perry, you help her up into the Caravelle, and out at the other end, and keep her happy on the way. Jonno and I have some aviation matters to discuss.'

'Yeah, I'm sure, you've got important things to fix. Anyway, let's find Benahid. A little nightcap, I think, before we hit the sack. Night Jonno.'

They ambled from the room and started along the corridor. The last sound Jonathan heard was a sudden noisy laugh from down there, somewhere about where the stairs began. It was Charlie of course. Charlie's eruption of a laugh – you had to smile when you heard it.

And he did smile, and with the smile still there, slipped off to sleep.

Two more 'Jonathan Kane' adventures by
Alexander Barrie :
Fly For Three Lives 45p

When Jonathan got a holiday job at Lonehead Flying Field he
expected a few enjoyable weeks of messing about with planes and
a couple of flying lessons.

But when the sinister Mr Barrington-Ward appeared, Jon was
suddenly launched into real airborne adventure — stolen planes,
flying bullets and a cut-throat crew of political gangsters.

Operation Midnight 45p

It seemed as if it would never stop raining at Lonehead Flying
Field. Then an urgent call from the Ministry of Defence plunged
Jonathan and the rest of the team into a new adventure.

'Operation Midnight' — the code name for a mission to Africa to
rescue Ephraim Demir from his border hideout. The mission became
more and more dangerous as Jonathan found himself at the centre
of a thrilling prison rescue.

There will be more !

Marie Herbert
Great Polar Adventures 40p

Eleven thrilling stories of men who risked their lives to get to the ends of the earth. The quest for the North and South Poles started as early as Elizabethan times but they have only been properly explored in the last few years. Wallie Herbert's story is included in this collection and you can plot the routes on the maps he has drawn.

Carey Miller
Submarines 40p

Hazardous missions, daring exploits and rescue operations are retold in this book of true submarine stories.

Carey Miller
Airships and Balloons 40p

Amazing tales of airships and balloons, from the one-man hot-air balloons of the 18th century to the huge hydrogen-filled Zeppelins of World War 1.

Arthur C. Clark
Dolphin Island 40p

This exciting story is set in the 21st century on an island in the Great Barrier Reef. Johnny, who has run away from home and hidden aboard an inter-continental hovership, is shipwrecked in the middle of the South Pacific Ocean. Stranded on a raft, he is miraculously propelled by a pack of dolphins towards the famous centre for dolphin research. Johnny is allowed to stay on the island and assist in training the dolphins. He goes skin diving at night, survives a fearful hurricane and unearths a horrifying underwater conspiracy.